THE LEGACY SERIES

Series Titles

Fugitive Daydreams
Leah McCormack

The Effects of Urban Renewal on Mid-Century America and Other Crime Stories
Jeff Esterholm

What Makes You Think You're Supposed to Feel Better
Jody Hobbs Hesler

Hoist House: A Novella & Stories
Jenny Robertson

Finding the Bones: Stories & A Novella
Nikki Kallio

Self-Defense
Corey Mertes

Where Are Your People From?
James B. De Monte

Sometimes Creek
Steve Fox

The Plagues
Joe Baumann

The Clayfields
Elise Gregory

Kind of Blue
Christopher Chambers

Evangelina Everyday
Dawn Burns

Township
Jamie Lyn Smith

Responsible Adults
Patricia Ann McNair

Great Escapes from Detroit
Joseph O'Malley

Nothing to Lose
Kim Suhr

The Appointed Hour
Susanne Davis

Praise for
Fugitive Daydreams

"McCormack's stories do nothing to protect anyone—especially the writer herself, and she is a writer, and a good one, and if what she writes sometimes makes you want to leave the room—as somehow you feel a terrific row is in the brewing, leaving is in fact impossible as any reader will have to know what happens next."

—Pete Dexter
author of *Paris Trout*
National Book Award winner

"These are riveting, inventive stories of attachment, separation, and fragmentation. I love the restless energy of this collection, and I admire its perfect fusion of urgency and playfulness. McCormack is a writer of great substance and style."

—Chris Bachelder
author of *The Throwback Special*
National Book Award finalist

"*Fugitive Daydreams* is an important and beautifully written book. The collection breaks new ground with the spellbinding way it subverts a reader's narrative expectations. In each narrative, McCormack's stare is unflinching. The last narrative is masterful, in its clear-eyed examination of a female artist's encounters with the overt and covert sexism, racism, and white male egomania embedded in all levels of the academic experience, both inside and outside of the classroom. The revelations, which are mostly cast as dramatic scenes, are courageously and brilliantly rendered. When I finished reading this unique collection, I thought, this is what an artist does."

—Patrick O'Keefe
author of *The Visitors* and *The Hill Road*
Story Prize winner

"Reading this poignant, uncanny, and unyielding collection, I was moved, unsettled, and gloriously angry. By turns furious, melancholy, and tender, these stories are gems."

—Leah Stewart
author of *What You Don't Know About Charlie Outlaw*

"Leah McCormack's *Fugitive Daydreams* is incredible—stylistically daring, formally inventive, emotionally raw, intellectually searching, it probes and proves what it is the short story can do. In McCormack's hands, it can entertain us, it can challenge us, it can change us. A remarkable, and remarkably brave first book."

—Brock Clarke
author of *Who Are You, Calvin Bledsoe?* and *I, Grape*

"A rhythmic work at once vulnerable yet pulsating with restrained persistence and brilliance. The narratives in this collection are America in all of its heartbreak and dirt, its grit, intractability, quiet desperation, unquiet desperation, and promise (also the promise of the failure of) occasional transcendence. One insightful fragment after another, under the overarching gravitas of the voice, takes hold of a reader and will not let go."

—Salar Abdoh
author of *A Nearby Country Called Love* and *Out of Mesopotamia*

"*Fugituve Daydreams* is a multifaceted marvel, an intricate hybrid of story, memoir, and literary criticism. Themes, characters, and situations—twins, sexism, alcoholism, travel, restlessness or disappointment in love and in jobs--keep recurring and deepening, and the book steadily accumulates emotional power and poignancy as it goes. By the end it morphs into something that's less a traditional 'collection of stories' than a spiky, questing, deeply personal novel. Fierce, vulnerable, thoughtful, laceratingly self-aware and other-aware—this is a debut that lingers in the mind long after one finishes reading."

—Michael Griffith
author of *Speaking Stone: Stories Cemeteries Tell*

"Leah McCormack's *Fugitive Daydreams* is inventive, comic, and—in the best way—weird, but its stylistic aerobatics aren't its greatest feat: it's how these twelve stories speak to the reader's beating heart. The dissection of a bizarre turn-of-the-century Christmas photograph subtly reveals the complexities of a contemporary family; a man's fixation with a gorilla illuminates the great gulf of desire in a doomed relationship. But the collection's recurring theme is how sickness can turn a family home into the strangest setting of all. Reminiscent of the work of Aimee Bender and Ottessa Moshfegh, this remarkable debut collection marks the arrival of a brilliant and intoxicating new voice."

—Marjorie Celona
author of *Y* and *How a Woman Becomes a Lake*

Fugitive Daydreams

STORIES

Leah McCormack

Cornerstone Press
Stevens Point, Wisconsin

Cornerstone Press, Stevens Point, Wisconsin 54481
Copyright © 2023 Leah McCormack
www.uwsp.edu/cornerstone

Printed in the United States of America by
Point Print and Design Studio, Stevens Point, Wisconsin

Library of Congress Control Number: 2023942179
ISBN: 978-1-960329-12-7

Cornerstone Press titles are produced in courses and internships offered by the Department of English at the University of Wisconsin–Stevens Point.

DIRECTOR & PUBLISHER   EXECUTIVE EDITOR
Dr. Ross K. Tangedal   Jeff Snowbarger

SENIOR EDITORS
Lexie Neeley, Monica Swinick, Kala Buttke

PRESS STAFF
Carolyn Czerwinski, Grace Dahl, Zoie Dinehart, Kirsten Faulkner, Brett Hill, Natalie Reiter, Arianna Soto, Chloe Verhelst

For Dietrik—
my destination and my home

Contents

Welcome, Welcome, Welcome. Come in. Come in. Come in.

Forget what you know about the beach house. Forget what you know about the condo. Forget what you know about the mansion and the cabin and the mobile home. The life of a house is hard. The house should know. It's been around for nearly two centuries. It's outstayed three separate families and is now housing its fourth, the Baxters. The truth, the house thinks, is that any type of house would give up its inhabitants, if it could.

But, alas: a house needs its inhabitants to run the water in its pipes, to heat its insides, to kill the termites and, at the very least, to save it from demolition—even if those same inhabitants clean nothing and fix nothing and throw stuff at its walls and kick in its doors and keep it awake all hours of the night with their screaming and cursing and crying and fucking.

The Baxters have lived in the house for more than thirty years. Before the Baxters moved in, the house was a farm-house. The shed in back was a chicken coop, the barn at the edge of the field filled with the bleating of sheep and goats and cows. Back then, the two-story house was treated to fresh coats of paint at least once every decade; its roof was replaced about a third as often, the siding too. The floors were mopped weekly, the shelves dusted, and the cobwebs removed from the ceilings. Ah, the good old days! the house would say, if it could.

But then the last old farmer died, and his wife moved away. The animals disappeared, and the crops went untended. The land was divided, and the house sold to a new family—the Baxters.

The house knows that the Baxters think that it would tell them, if it could, how it has grown attached to them, looks after them, maybe even loves them. How their son is like its own son, the mother and the father its best friends. But the house is not a good liar. And, anyway, the house, being a house, cannot talk with the family it houses. It can only watch. It can only listen.

But the house is smart. It picks up on things.

The house has read the faces of the Baxters when they look up at the house or open the front door and step inside. It knows that the Baxters wouldn't miss it, either.

Lately the mother is always home and usually alone. All day long she sits on the couch in the living room and watches the made-for-TV movies that the house has come to despise. It isn't that the house minds the mother, per se. It isn't the smell of her farts or the unsightly manner in which she clutches her crotch as she clomps to the bathroom. And it isn't that she pees herself, despite the clutching, or that she continues to wear the pee-soaked pants all day long, leaving butt prints on the couch and chairs. It isn't even the moldy smell that emanates from her lap three days later when she's still wearing the pants. No, it isn't any of *these* things the house minds. What the house minds is the mother's loneliness. It minds the way her eyes feed off the clock. It minds her Silly-Putty face that crumples and sobs without warning and then smooths out again by the end of a commercial. It minds her obsession with keeping the cordless phone, the phone that never rings, next to her on the table beside the couch. And it minds the stray dog that she's adopted to keep her company. The dog with the tumor on its back and the half-paw that—the house overheard one day—was lopped off by a bear trap.

The house wants to yell at the mother: To hell with this sitting in front of the TV and eating chips and drinking beer! To hell with this waiting! Get up! *Do* something!

But the house knows better. It knows that the mother's growing fascination with bad TV has something to do with the needles (*Copaxone*: the house reads one day) that she stocks in the fridge and uses to prick her thigh every morning before her husband leaves for work. The house has noted over the years how her right arm has curled in towards her chest. How her right leg scrapes forward like a loosely-hinged door.

Sometimes the house wonders how the father could let the stacks of newspapers and broken TVs and lamps and picture frames pile up in the kitchen and living room—how, when he must see what the house sees: the sharp edges, the rusty metal, the broken glass. Each time the mother loses her balance and crashes to the floor (just barely missing another sharp edge), and no one is home to help her back up, the house wishes the son would return. The son would know to clear the house. Like before, he would make things bearable.

Seeing the mother like this gets the house thinking. And for the first time in its life, the house wonders how long it has left to live. But the house doesn't know any other houses, and so it has no point of reference from which to make such a guess. It has never heard anyone talk about the life expectancy of a house on TV. Certainly the Baxters never talk about it. And it isn't as if the house has legs to stand up and walk over to the barn: Hey, Barn. How long you got left to live? What about Shed over there—how long you think Shed's got?

So the house figures it out for itself. It figures it has loads more years left to live. Heck, it's in the prime of its life! Bring on another century!

The house is just kidding. It isn't a fool. That its floorboards now sink with each footstep hasn't escaped its attention. That it can hear the wind whistling through its walls and feel the water dripping from the pipes in its basement is no small thing to the house. And it knows what the stain on the ceiling of the son's old bedroom means.

The house has conceived of a hundred schemes for getting the father upstairs to look at the brown stain, but the man can't seem to grasp the simplest hint. And, anyway, the house knows that even if the father does see the stain, he will only mope and whine about it, about how he has no time or money to fix a leaky roof; and it will not be until the son comes home—which happens so rarely these days—that any work gets done on the roof.

And the house, being a house, knows what a leaky roof can do to a house if it is not fixed immediately. The house can see it in its mind already: the wood in the roof growing soft with rot and the rain and snow dripping down into the walls, spreading—Oh! what frustration the house feels! To go to a doctor and say I have cancer, and to have the doctor fumble around and take a year to agree, Yes, you have cancer, and then to ask the doctor, Will we go immediately to surgery then, remove the tumor? and to have to sit there and wait for the doctor's answer, wait weeks and months and years, the tumor growing larger and larger all the while, a grape to a baseball to a cantaloupe, and then to finally have the damn doctor tell you, Okay: Let's operate, when the cancer has already spread to the liver and the lymph nodes and the marrow and what the hell is the point now!

This sort of thing never happens on *ER*, the house considers.

One day the house hears the mother telling the father that their son Tom is bringing his fiancé home for a visit. The mother's eyes are vibrant. This is a big deal: the house gets that right away. For the mother's sake (and the house's sake) the house hopes the visit goes well. It cannot bear the thought of spending another depressing day alone with the mother. And, too, the house has faith that the son will find and fix the leaky roof.

If it weren't for him, the house knows, it would have crumbled long ago.

As the big weekend approaches, however, the house—much to its surprise—grows more and more anxious. For days it watches the mother and the father and waits. A week passes, two, and now it panics. The house is not prepared for the fiancé's visit! It is cluttered with junk and dusty with dirt and stinking of old garbage. The toilet bowl upstairs is glazed with a film of dried feces, the tub green with slime. The front door is an old blanket tacked to the doorframe.

The house wants to scream at the father: Replace the door already! Scream at the mother: Clean something! Scream at them both: What is wrong with you!

Finally, the house sees what it has become. It has become a recluse. And it cannot imagine a worse fate for a house. It is as if the house blinked, and the world changed in that instant, the house wishing now that it had legs so that it could run up the stairs and hide like Tom used to do whenever someone knocked on the front door.

But, of course, the house, being a house, has no legs to run and hide.

The house is wracked with worry. It is constantly on edge. When the phone on the table by the couch comes abruptly to life one afternoon, the house is nearly as startled by it as the mother. By the time she finally connects the source of the ringing to the phone and picks it up, though, the house has calmed itself enough to listen.

From the mother's remarks, the house gathers that it is Tom calling to say that he has changed his plans. He will not be bringing his fiancé with him this weekend, will not be coming home at all. "What about next Saturday?" the mother suggests. "Oh. I see." She listens for a while, her head drooping into her chest. "No, no, I understand."

At first, although the house is greatly relieved, it feels sorry for the mother. It knows how much she has been looking forward to the visit.

But then it hears her later that day talking with the father in the kitchen.

"You know what it is?" she says. "It's this goddamn house!" Her upper lip curls back and she thrusts a menacing hand at the ceiling. "He's ashamed of this filthy goddamn house!"

For weeks afterwards, the house cannot bear to face the mother on the couch. The same scene plays out in its mind again and again: the mother raising her good fist at the house, accusing it, threatening it. The house feels deeply insulted. It longs to set that woman straight. To set all the Baxters straight. If only the house could speak, it would have plenty to say, plenty. But, of course, the house, being a house, cannot speak to the family it houses.

So the house composes a letter instead.

Dear Baxters:

In light of recent events, the house feels the need to point out a few things to you Baxters. First of all—and the house really must stress this—it wasn't the house who spray painted "Tom is a bafoon [sic]"on the front of the house (and didn't bother to paint over it these last ten years). The house didn't decide to save $25 a month by canceling the town's garbage pick-up service so that the black bags now pile up on the front lawn, waiting every few months to be brought to the dump. And as long as it's on the subject of garbage, the house would also like to point out that it—a mere house—cannot be held responsible for the fortnightly spilling of the rancid garbage juice all over the kitchen floor nor, for that matter, for the maggots that crawl out of the overflowing trash bin and up the walls and hang from the ceiling (or for the one that dropped into Tom's hair while he was eating a bowl of Cheerios years ago).

Second, the house has never thrown a plate of spaghetti marinara or a bottle of wine or ketchup against its walls. (If it had thrown them, it would have at least bothered to clean up afterward—at some point.) The house has never kicked a hole in its wall, pulled a door off its hinges, or flipped a table upside down and stomped on it until it was a pile of splintered wood. And while the house is sorry that Tom's first—and only—high-school girlfriend wouldn't sit or use the toilet or eat dinner during her visit and broke up with him the next day, the house is not responsible for that, either. The house would like to remind the Baxters that the house, being a house, cannot pick up broom or

Welcome, Welcome, Welcome. Come in. Come in. Come in.

vacuum or mop or sponge or scrubber, cannot wield hammer or nail or paintbrush.

So: if you Baxters need the house to be your scapegoat, the house has no choice but to be your scapegoat. But so far as the house is concerned, when and if Tom ever returns for a visit, he can cry all he wants when he discovers that the washcloth he uses to clean his face has also become his mother's rag for removing the father's diarrhea from the toilet seat. The house doesn't care. The house doesn't set the booby traps. It doesn't pull the pots and pans covered in mouse turds from the cabinets and cook dinner without cleaning them. It isn't the house who pees itself and leaves butt prints all over the furniture. The house doesn't insist on keeping company with a mangy, stinky cripple of a dog. In fact, if it could, the house would make a point to get out of the house every once in a while (unlike someone else the house could name).

Yours Truly,
House

But, of course, the house, being a house, cannot write down nor deliver a letter to the family it houses. It can only watch. It can only listen. It can only think.

After the house finishes composing the letter, it has plenty of time to think. And this is what it thinks: the Baxters are from another planet. It is the only explanation. For the house has heard the mother and father tell Tom about a place called "Indiana" where they were supposedly raised in nice suburban homes. And yet they both behave as if they have no idea what it means to a sixteen-year-old boy to bring his girlfriend home to this squalor, the names he will be called at school…but that was—what?—fifteen years ago. The house still recalls spying on Tom and his girlfriend in the upstairs bedroom. How he'd held her as she stood in the center of the room and asked, in a daze, why the barn was nicer than the house and refused his invitations to take a seat.

Yes, the house knows a thing or two from TV about suburbia. Things the mother, an avid TV watcher now, should also know—but apparently *still* doesn't.

Just when the house thinks things can't get any worse, Tom comes home.

Right away he follows his father upstairs to the old bedroom, and the two of them examine the stain. The house is shocked: How did the father know the stain was there? Perhaps, the house thinks, it has underestimated the father.

For the first time in what feels like a very long time, the house is hopeful.

The next evening, Tom clambers up a ladder and stomps on the slanted roof in his steel-toe boots, testing the shingles. A boot sinks into the mossy roof, and he wrenches his heel free from the hole and climbs back down the ladder. He goes inside and gets a beer and comes back out and stands in the porch doorway drinking his Schlitz and gazing at the overgrown lawn. Then he walks across the yard, tossing the empty can over his shoulder into the bushes, and goes into the shed. When he reemerges, he is carrying a rolled-up tarp.

He climbs back up the ladder with the limp tube balanced on his shoulder. On the roof, he snaps the blue plastic open and covers the hole.

"How's it going?" the father calls from down below. "I can't see a thing."

Tom pulls a nail gun from his tool belt and secures a corner of the tarp. "Almost done!"

Welcome, Welcome, Welcome. Come in. Come in. Come in.

Before the sun has set, Tom is back in his car and waving goodbye to the mother and the father and the house and the cheap blue tarp.

The house knows that Tom will not return to finish the roof: the roof is finished.

And so is the house.

The house has settled down with the mangy dog, the Hallmark Channel and Tori Spelling. It has forgotten the hole in the roof and the tarp nailed to its shingles. It has forgotten Tom and the mother and the father and its letter to the Baxters. The house has discovered how easy it is to forget these things, how easy it is to hide. Occasionally it feels the wind tug at the tarp on the roof and is reminded of its exposed rafters—but then *Oprah* comes on, and it forgets again.

* * *

When at last the soft ripple of gravel turning under tires rouses the house, there is no way for it to know how much time has passed. The house looks for the mother for answer, but she is not on the couch. It looks again: she is not in any of the beds, either. Finally, the house sees the father outside. He is leaning on a cane—But wait! the house thinks. That isn't the father.

The house looks more carefully at the man. Can it be?

Oh, but it is! It's the house! The house is standing right there, on its own two legs, leaning on the cane and waving its free hand. Waving, it now sees, to its previous inhabitants, all the farmers and their families, crowded inside the cabin of an approaching tractor. The house cannot wait to pick the children up in its arms and hug the parents.

For you, the house would say, if it could. It was all for you.

And then the house hears something it has never heard before. The house hears its own voice. "Welcome," it says and stumbles forward. "Welcome," it says, and its knees begin to buckle. "Welcome," it says and falls to the ground. "Come in. Come in. Come in."

95359

Are little boys supposed to sit atop reindeer? In no Christmas carol I've ever heard is there a child perched on a reindeer. But this animal looks more like a Shetland pony or a donkey—maybe it *is* a pony. It has something of the circus about it, like it wishes it'd die already. That Santa is no Santa I'd ever put a kid near, let alone on the knee of, as is now the custom in most malls in America. Thank god for the suicidal pony. But maybe it's a stuffed pony-reindeer. Maybe it's a stuffed Santa. The window, come to think of it, looks like cardboard cutout and kraft paper. I believe in this Santa, though, more than I do in the boy. Picture the kid walking in those stiff rubber boots that rise above the knees—can't be done. Notice we can't even tell if he's a *whole* boy, with two legs. Even the far hand looks like an inflated rubber glove. And that riding crop—is there some perverted message here? On the back of the photo someone has written "1910." My father tells me this must be a photo of his father. Does he mean Santa or the boy? If he's my grandfather, then 95359 is an Irish address. A real address or make believe, I don't know. Behind the door could be a bunch of Irish elves hammering into place the heads of dolls and spokes of wooden cars. But probably you can't even open the door, a structure props it up, and to the side of it, outside our view, waits a line of children and parents. Do they find this Santa creepy or is he the standard? Is there an onlooker somewhere chuckling behind his hand at the spectacle? The boy, the crop, the letch. But what if my grandfather is Santa? It's possible: my father has that sharp nose, those light, dark-lashed eyes. He wears winter caps and boots year-round, sometimes lets his beard grow out. It's starting to gray. Do I care, being related to a pederast? Should I be held in some way accountable for his actions, this man I never met and only ever saw in a single photograph? What about the boy? What about his descendants—do I owe them anything? Will my future children and grandchildren owe them and theirs? Where does it end? Or, okay, Santa's not my ancestor. Now I'm descended from a victim of sodomy. Don't feel bad for me—I didn't feel a thing. Or maybe my father meant the pony. Maybe that's my father's father. Resemblance: uncanny. Right now, in fact, reading this, my father's head droops in disappointment. Disappointed with what, I don't know—life? So, okay, his father left behind his homeland and its creepy scenarios, like the one portrayed here. He misses his family, his friends, the neighbor girl he's always loved. But come winter, what does he find? Santa. On street corners and in stores and outside churches. No shortage of jobs for the man, no shortage of knees for the boy. So, what's disappointing, I ask you. Unless it's for the Shetland pony that my father bows his head. Oh yes, the pony.

There Are Worse Things

Every time my family gets together, it's the same thing. At some point, Mom—or *Betty*—lashes out at her daughter-in-law for no discernible reason, while the rest of us, embarrassed, tell her to shut up and call her crazy. Usually by then the five of us are packed into the living room of Jack and Karen's tiny apartment in Chicago, their dog sniffing the coffee table, knocking over empty cans of Milwaukee's Best, and Betty is halfway through her second glass of boxed merlot.

Look-it, Karen, she might start, don't tell *me* [etc., etc.]—and before we know it, her voice turns into a screeching balloon. Strands of gray hair whip her face with each vitriolic word. Then Jack and I yell, Mom! Mom! Stop! What the hell are you doing? Mom! until Dad's voice rolls over us like a rusty oil drum:

Betty! You uncouth! Spiteful! Bitch!

At which point, we leave him to the hysterical cripple and head to a bar to share a pitcher of beer and reassure Karen: It has nothing to do with you. She's nuts.

Neither of us, Jack nor I, ever mentions MS.

I did once, about a year ago, something like: It's not her fault, it's the MS.

But Karen cut me off: Betty knows what she's doing.

And Jack agreed, claimed it had nothing to do with MS. She'd always been tactless, had always been a liar.

This was news to me, my mother lying. But Jack, seven years my senior, insisted: Mom used to lie to me when I was a kid. Even then, he said, I could tell. She's manipulative.

You don't think her mind's been affected by the MS? I argued. What about her memory? It gets worse every year. If you went home—

Memory loss, Karen said, is no excuse for meanness.

I knew what she really meant. Her mother had recently had an emergency brain operation that resulted in a total loss of her short-term memory. Compared to her, Betty was a genius.

Unlike Karen's mother last week, for instance, Betty at least remembers why our family has gotten together this weekend: Jack and Karen have a newborn.

All throughout her own parents' stay, Karen confides in me late the first night of our visit, her mother kept squinting at the baby and gasping: Whose is *that*?

I wish, Karen tells me, her eyes glazed from drinking but fixed on the crib in the corner, I wish my mother were still my mother. I always pictured her helping me when I had a baby. You can't imagine what it's like—losing your mother, her memory gone.

Gee, I say dryly, glancing at the empty Busch cans on the coffee table; at Jack, passed out on the sofa beside Karen; at the mashing and stretching of pink flesh taking place inside her transparent electric breast pumps. Gosh. I guess I can't.

Earlier that Friday evening, when my parents and I had arrived from Albany and followed Jack into the kitchen, Karen held up the baby: Our son. Isn't he cute?

We circled around her and stared at the blob of flesh.

Let me hold him! Betty said, having—I knew from her nagging me over the years—looked forward to cradling her first grandchild ever since Jack was born, nearly four decades earlier. Let me hold him, she said and stumbled forward, her good arm raised. Give him here.

Karen pulled the baby closer to her chest.

Mom, Jack said, why don't you sit down? You must be tired from the trip.

I'm not tired! Mike wouldn't even let me walk through the airport.

Dad muttered: She asked the attendant for the wheelchair.

Betty, Karen said, her voice taking on the firm, patient tone of a new mother. If you sit down, I can hold him in your lap. There's no reason to get upset.

Now, hours later, tired and longing to join my parents in the bedroom where my sleeping bag waits for me on floor, I tell Karen: I couldn't possibly imagine what it's like to have a mother like that. No memory. Gee, I add for effect. Wow.

It's sad, she agrees. Even her personality is different. She cracks jokes now.

At least, I say, she's still alive. Didn't the surgery save her life?

Karen says nothing. Her eyes follow the white liquid moving from her breasts through the plastic tubes into the bottle in her lap: an alcohol dump, she explained to me earlier. So Baby can suck on Mama's fun bags tomorrow without getting drunk.

What about the rest of us? Karen says. What about our lives?

(Karen's mother had a ruptured brain aneurysm. Now she has severe cognitive impairment.

Gone, short term memory.

Gone, whatever it is that made Karen think: This is my mother.)

By noon the next day, Jack is in the kitchen filling a sports bottle with boxed merlot while Karen tucks the baby inside her Moby Wrap, Dad feeds the dog, and I yell: Come on, Mom! Let's get you outside. About half an hour ago, we decided to see a Matisse retrospective at the Art Institute of Chicago, because: Why the hell not? At least we'd get out of the apartment.

It takes Betty and me fifteen minutes to descend the flight of stairs and cross the street to the minivan on the curb, and by the time she's let go of my arm and flumped into the passenger seat, Jack is already behind the wheel and jamming his sports bottle into the cup holder. Before I can close Betty's door and join Karen and Dad in back,

Shit, she mumbles. I have to pee.

Why didn't you go before we left? I grumble.

I didn't have to then.

Betty has to pee! I announce. She didn't go before we left!

You'd better hold it, Jack says, raising the sports bottle to his lips. Or pee in the seat.

Jack! Karen says. She can't pee in our van.

Never mind, Betty says. I'll wait until we get to the museum.

At the Art Institute, Jack heads over to security and gets Betty a wheelchair. When he returns, he tells her: We could have a lot more fun this weekend if you had one of these—go to Millennium Park, check out the pier. Too bad you left it at home.

It wouldn't fit in the trunk, she says and plops her wet bottom onto the chair.

That's not true, Dad interrupts. You didn't want to bring it.

Mike… she says between her teeth.

Jack scoffs and shakes his head and pushes Betty through the busy hallway to the ladies' room, the rest of us following close behind. He deposits her in the entrance tunnel, then: Marian, he says, waving me to the chair, and walks off towards the men's room.

I don't have to pee anymore, Betty tells me as I grab the handles.

I know, I say, backing out of the entrance. Behind us, the baby starts to wail.

Last night, before waking Jack and pulling out the sofa bed, Karen asked: Why did this have to happen to my mother, of all people? She's never been anything but kind. It makes you wonder. Like, what's the point?

I stared at her chugging breasts. Hmm, I said.

Karen slumped. I'm so—she gritted her teeth—angry. Why *her*?

As opposed, I said, to whom?

Now, in the elevator at the Art Institute, she snaps: Haven't you had enough?

Don't be a hypocrite, Jack says, returning the bottle to the inside pocket of his coat.

Karen rubs the bulge tied to her chest, sighs.

Betty swivels her gray head around in the chair. What's that smell?

Careful, Dad jokes, his voice tense. You'll get her drunk off the fumes.

What fumes? Betty says, and the doors open. Jack elbows me out of the way. Give her here, he says, and takes hold of the wheelchair.

A year ago—only a few weeks before Jack announced that Karen was pregnant—I took a bus out of Port Authority and spent that Saturday, my birthday, with my parents. Though they live only a couple of hours from Brooklyn, I rarely visit. Going back home depresses me. I'm reminded of all the things I've lost. And all the things I've failed to gain. That time, it was my thirtieth. Finding Betty now anchored in front of the TV, I felt death everywhere.

How are things with what's-his-name? she asked during a commercial break. Think you'll marry this one?

We broke up, I said and felt the cake I was chewing lodge in my throat.

Oh. She lifted a can of Schlitz from the couch arm and sipped. You know, Marian. Lots of women these days are raising children on their own, without a husband. I wish I had.

Mom, I said. Dad can hear you. He's in the kitchen.

Well? she said. So?

Behind me, I heard Dad: Thanks, honey! Love you, too.

What I mean is, she continued, there's no reason to wait for someone special. Get yourself knocked up, go it alone— before it's too late. Best thing I ever did was have you kids.

I put my plate of cake down. I'm not that old.

Honey, I didn't—

What's so great about being a mother? I said, thinking: God, please, don't let me turn out like her, rotting alone on a couch.

Shit. Her head flopped back into the pillow propped up against the wall. Shit.

Jack and Karen, I offered, might still have a baby. She's not too old.

Karen? Christ. She picked the can back up, looked at the TV. You'll regret it, Marian.

Every Matisse painting in the exhibit is surrounded by at least half a dozen heads. Yet when I find Jack and Betty studying a painting of a blue room with two goldfish in a glass bowl, they're the only people near the canvas. Seeing me, Jack's lips part into a purple smile and he whispers: Look how well he captures the shape of the fish. It's just two blobs of orange, but they're *alive*, swimming. Then he exclaims, for others: This guy can't paint worth shit!

A few people turn sharply, and, at the sight of the old woman in the wheelchair, pause.

Oh, Jack! Betty says. You're too much!

He bursts into laughter. And, just as abruptly, stops.

I want to see *that* one! Betty points across the room. Bring me over there!

She's been bossing me like this, Jack complains, ever since we got here. Then he bends over her shoulder and comes up with the sports bottle. He takes a slug from the green plastic, then drops it in her lap, and pushes the wheelchair to the painting.

Excuse me, he says, nudging the chair into the backs of knees and thighs. Excuse me, he says, ignoring the glares. Excuse me, he says, coming to a stop, just as Betty's shoes hit the wall.

Oh. She gazes up at the nude. We've seen this one already.

Jack laughs. Sure we have, Betty.
Yeah.

Just like the goldfish.
Yeah.

(Karen's mother's brain was surrounded by blood. On my mother's brain there are lesions.)

Back on the first floor, Jack returns from his second trip to the men's room inspired. Give her here, he tells Dad. Then commandeers wheelchair-plus-Betty across the blonde oak to the glass doors.

Shit, Karen says. Shit, shit.

Dad looks at me and says, Stop him.

I stride after them. But only just in time to hear: Jack! The chair! Don't forget—

Jesus, Mom, he croaks, eyeing the security guard. Keep your voice down.

They exit unnoticed and, in a matter of seconds, have zipped down the wheelchair ramp, hit pavement, and entered the park.

You idiot! Karen says over the top of Baby's fabric-wrapped head when we approach Jack in the parking garage. He's cramming the wheelchair into the trunk of the rusty Plymouth Voyager. You'd better bring that chair back—now!

His head pops up, and he turns. Bring it *back*?

What if they caught you on their security cameras?

He considers this a moment. Then looks at the rest of us. Didn't we need this thing? for Mom? Betty, he calls through the hatchback to the passenger seat, you wanted the chair, right?

Whatever you want, honey.

Jack, Karen says. You could go to jail for this.

He scratches his neck, looks at the chair's black wheels hanging out over the bumper. Fuck it, he says. It doesn't fit in the van, anyway.

On the way back from the museum, Jack pulls into a Jewel parking lot, and he and Karen climb out of the van to buy dinner and beer and a two-liter of soda for Dad, who hollers from the last row of seats as the doors slide shut: Sprite, diet!

Karen gives him a sharp look through the window, puts a finger to her lips, and points at Baby strapped into his car seat, asleep.

Sorry, Dad mouths, embarrassed.

Don't worry, I say. If the museum noise didn't bother him, that sure as hell won't.

From the passenger seat: You said it, Marian!

Then the baby starts to cry.

Shit, I say. Shit. And glance out the window: Karen is gone, sucked into the bowels of the supermarket. Dad! I say, elbowing him in his big gut. Do something.

I can't, he says, exasperated, and shifts uncomfortably in the seat. I can't get up.

Oh my God, I say, covering my ears. I lean over the seat and look at Baby's crumpled red face. Shh, I say, rubbing his stomach. Shh, there, there. But the wailing turns into shrieking.

Betty opens her door, drops one leg out and then the other, leans against the doorframe, stands. I slide the back door open, and she ducks her head into the van. You've had a long day, she coos to Screaming Baby. Unbuckle him, she instructs me from the door. Pick him up.

I struggle to get the squishy limbs free of the straps, then am lifting Baby by the armpits, my fingers supporting his head, and floating him over to Betty.

You hold him, she says.

I pause, Baby dangling midair, mouth a cave of anguish. Then I pull him into my chest.

Like this?

Try to bounce him a little, she says and smiles. That's right.

The van is suddenly quiet.

Holy shit, I whisper. You're a genius, Mom.

Last year, not long after I'd celebrated my thirtieth, I called home. Congratulations! I said after my father put me on speaker phone.

What do you mean? Mom shouted from the next room. Didn't Jack tell you?

Yes, Dad said. Betty, you remember. Karen's pregnant.

Oh! Betty yelled. Yeah, he told us that.

I waited for her to say something else. So…, I said. Grandparents.

Yes, Dad said. We're thrilled.

Uh-huh, Mom chimed in. Then, raising her voice again: How are you, Marian?

I'm fine, I said impatiently.

We're just watching the Mets here, Mom said. Not much to report.

Yeah, I can hear it in the background. When did Jack call you?

Last night, Dad said. Took us by surprise. Right, Betty? Yeah.

Goddamn it! he said. Get off the couch and come in here and talk to Marian.

She can hear me fine! Right, Marian? Oh, Mike! Where the—where are you going? Mike! Oh, for Christ's…!

Then I heard her shuffling into the kitchen.

Hi, Mom. Did Dad just leave the house?

Yep.

Boy, I said dryly, do I ever miss being home. And wondered what was worse: the noise of that house or the silence of my efficiency apartment.

Then I asked her, Why aren't you excited about the baby?

I *am* excited. She picked up the phone, sighed. I don't know. It's not the same.

What do you mean?

Karen won't want my help.

That's not true, I said, even though I guessed it probably was. You can still help, I said, and wondered how, with her disabilities.

No, it's not the same. It's not like when your own daughter is pregnant.

It's still a big deal, I snapped, your first grandchild.

Oh yes. I know—of course. She paused. You're smart, Marian. You have a career, your own life. All I ever wanted were kids, a family.

That's not true, I said, thinking of the jobs she had when I was a teenager, jobs from which she had been fired due to "incompetence" and other dubious reasons. You worked, I said.

Just to help support the family. The jobs themselves weren't rewarding. But you—

Oh boy, I said, a curator. And suddenly I felt horrifyingly empty. That isn't, I said, what I envisioned for myself when I got my MFA.

Yes, well. There are worse things.

When Jack and Karen return from the grocery store to find Baby in my lap, I tell them: As soon as you left, he started crying. Mom helped soothe him.

Karen looks at Betty in the passenger seat. Thanks.

Marian put him to sleep, not me.

I look down at the rubbery flesh stuffed into its onesie—and notice, for the first time, the black lashes on the closed lids, the stubby nose, pink lips. Soon, I realize, the fact hitting me like something big and obvious but only now visible, soon this thing will be a little person.

He looks, I tell Jack as he tears open a twelve-pack, like a miniature version of you.

Let's hope that's all he's inherited, Dad quips, eyeing Jack as he twists off a bottle cap. The family's good looks. Karen, you aren't Irish, are you?

Ha-ha, Jack says. Funny. Then he slams the rest of his beer for spite.

Sure, Mike, Betty shoots over her shoulder, it's always my genes you blame. The kids inherited a lot of shitty qualities from you, too.

(At thirty, Betty had an MRI.

Here, the doctor told her, pointing to a white marble in what appeared to be an x-ray of a head of gray cabbage. Here and here, he said. These are lesions. There will probably be more.)

She has lucid and not so lucid moments, I once explained of Betty to a boyfriend. She can say something that cuts straight to your heart one minute, and stare at you blankly the next, baffled by the simplest of explanations—but she pretends otherwise, won't admit her confusion.

It must be frightening, the boyfriend said, his eyes fixed on the ceiling.

For whom? I asked.

Now, several years and boyfriends later, as I sit in a booth at a bar with my brother while we once again reassure Karen, I'm reminded of that post-coital chat.

Who the hell knows, Jack says, what goes on inside Betty's head, why she does anything.

But she was so mean, Karen says. How can I not take it personally?

Jack and I stare into our pints of beer.

She's jealous, Jack finally suggests. She's upset and jealous, seeing you with the baby.

Only an hour previously, having returned from the Art Institute with our groceries, eaten hot dogs, and sat in the living room drinking, Jack was instructing Dad: If he cries, he's hungry or needs to be changed. Let Dad do it, Betty. We'll be back in a few hours.

I can change him.

Sure, Mom. But let Dad do it.

Then he went to the kitchen to grab a road soda, and Karen said: Here, Mike. I'm putting the diapers here. There are some bottles of breast milk in the fridge. We'll be around the corner. If you need us, call—

You look sexy, Betty snarled. All dressed up, woo-wee!

Betty, Dad warned. What the hell are you doing?

Hot to trot, fun times, that Karen!

Mom, I said, getting up from the couch, don't be crazy.

Crazy Betty, Crazy Betty! She struggled forward in her seat, her good arm flailing, and accidentally kicked the dog. It yelped and ran out of the room. Boy, she said, boy, I wish *I* could be sexy! Running around in that skimpy skirt! Drinking up a storm!

Karen stood in shock.

What the fuck, Mom! I grabbed her arms. Stop!

Crazy Betty! Crazy—!

I clapped a hand over her mouth, muffling her *Betty!*

Jack came back into the room, his pockets stuffed with cans of beer. He took one look at the mouth-clapped, red-faced Betty, her head still shaking violently, and said: Oh, shit.

Last night, while her breasts chugged away, Karen confessed to me: Sometimes I wish my mom didn't have the surgery. It'd be so much easier if she . . . if she wasn't . . .

You know who I feel bad for? she says tonight, as Jack and I sit with her in the booth. Your dad. He has to deal with Betty every day.

That's right, Jack says.

Uh-huh, I mumble, thinking of Betty's steamy breath on my palm.

I worry for my dad, Karen says. My mom forgets what happened minutes earlier, then yells at him when he tells her she's already done something, doesn't need to call so-and-so. She accuses him of lying, gets violent—*my* mother, the nicest person. And after he's calmed her down, there she is again, five minutes later, yelling at him about it all over again. The same thing, again and again, on and on.

Jack nods. That would, he says, test anyone's patience.

The same thing, Karen says through tears, again and again, day after day.

Wow, I say, as if hearing her for the first time. I can't imagine.

The next morning, our last in Chicago, I get up to pee, and find Betty sitting on a chair in front of a silent TV, holding a bottle to the baby's mouth.

Shh, she says and nods at Karen and Jack, passed out on the sofa bed. He kept them up all night, she says, then smiles and hands me the empty bottle. Get him another, would you?

If Betty remembers her tirade, I can't tell. Whole worlds, it seems, revolve all around me, outside my senses, all the time.

Then it occurs to me: What if she drops him? I whisk him off her lap.

His head bangs the back of the chair, and he starts wailing.

Give him to me, she says, her eyes flaring. You don't know what you're doing.

I do, too, I say, the baby sagging in my arms, his screams growing sharper. At the sight of Karen leaping from the sofa, I pull him into my chest. There, there, I try. Then I feel his weight being lifted off me and transferred into Karen's arms.

My mother fixes me with a look of profound disappointment.

No, dear, she says. You don't.

On my mother's brain there are lesions. There will be more.

Waiting

My lover has taken my tongue. He put it on the night table. Every night we go to sleep, and there it is, the tongue, floating in a jar of formaldehyde. I like to think this is because my lover intends one day to unscrew the cap and return my tongue to me. He says it's for the smell, to prevent rot.

The tongue is mottled pink and gray and looks like a giant slug. Even if my lover won't say that the tongue could be mine again, he hasn't thrown it away. More than a year has passed, and it is still in the jar on the table. I can't help but think it watches us while we sleep. If I could, I'd have a conversation with the tongue. Ask it what it sees.

Even before my tongue was taken, I'd noticed it wasn't working properly. Certain words, my brain would command the tongue to form them, but it'd lay flat, unmoving. Words like *baby, marriage*—it refused to shape the sounds. It'd push off the back of my front teeth, "Let's…" and go limp. My lover would look up from whatever he was doing: "Well?" Eventually other words, safe words, I don't know why—they sent the same panic signal to the tongue. It got to the point I couldn't trust the tongue at all anymore.

Nights I can't sleep, I look up at the tongue and wonder whether it's better off now. Does it feel safe in that jar? Perhaps it's selfish, my wanting it back. The tongue, anyway, has given no sign that it misses me. Do I expect it to curl itself into the shape of a heart? I don't know. This is what I know: I miss my tongue.

Once, I couldn't stand it any longer. I waited to hear the grinding of my lover's teeth (a sign that he was no longer conscious) and then twisted off the lid and plunged my hand deep into the cold. I slapped that fat sucker back into my mouth, where it belonged, and waited to hear its sweet sounds. But the tongue lay flat in my mouth like a dead fish.

Now my nights are filled with waiting. I study my lover's face, the dark eyebrows, plump cheeks. He's beautiful. Sweet when he sleeps. One day he will remember to return my tongue to me. My voice will come to him in a dream, and he'll think: I miss that voice. This is what it will take to turn the dead fish back into a tongue.

In the meantime, whole nights my lover sleeps, undisturbed. Tonight, as loudly as I can, I think: *Wake up.* I stare at him. *Wake up!* When he doesn't stir, I give his shoulder a shove. His lids slide back, and he stares at me. I offer my brightest smile—to match his vinyl record eyes—and he bolts up in bed, tearing the sheet off me. His back rises out of the mattress like a silent moon. It reminds me of the first time I told him I loved him.

Finally, he sinks back onto the bed. Closes his eyes. The teeth start grinding.

This is how we spend our nights: The tongue floats in the jar. My lover lies on his back on the bed. I hug the wall. He doesn't like when I touch him, my lover. Says he can't sleep with my body that close. So I don't touch him. I don't touch him, and I don't talk. I never remind him of the things he doesn't like to be reminded of. I used to remind him— when I had a tongue. I talked and talked and talked about writing. He doesn't like to be reminded about writing. He's a writer himself, struggling, like me, to write. I reminded him about writing, and I reminded him of him. He didn't like to be reminded of him. "We're going to end up hating each other," he told me once, "we're too much alike." I'm not as sophisticated as him. I thought being alike was a good thing. But it was painful for him, I knew. So I tried to be less like me.

My lover is indecisive, I'm indecisive. Before, if he asked where we should go for dinner, my mind would melt like butter. Now, I'd grab the neck of the first restaurant name that came to me and squeeze with both hands: *Grimaldi's!* Such conviction, you wouldn't believe. My lover didn't believe. He looked at me, disappointed, and suggested a different place.

On the phone: "What are you doing?" my lover would ask. And because I was reading or writing or reading about writing and didn't want to cause him unnecessary pain by reminding him of these things, I'd grunt. Then change the subject. "What are you doing?"

"Reading," he said. "Writing."

I waited for him to say more. He didn't.

A great big nothing filled the phone.

It wasn't the tongue's fault, I admit. The problems it had working properly—they can be traced back to me. My lover isn't much of a talker. I'm not much of a talker. From the beginning, silence threatened us. So I started talking. I talked about writing. I talked about struggles with writing. I talked about fears surrounding writing. I talked about reading that inspired writing. It was on my mind. It was on his mind. That was the trouble. Listening to me talk, he said, it was like listening to himself talk. He didn't want to listen to himself talk. He was sick of himself.

I wondered if that meant he was sick of me.

After I stopped talking about writing, there wasn't much for me to talk about. But I kept talking. Things I cared nothing about—whole conversations were made of this stuff.

We floated for a while, my lover and I, in this stew of words. Our love seemed to grow and grow. And before I knew it, as if my brain were out to sabotage me, sabotage *us*, our love—it started challenging the tongue. Demanding it say certain words. And at the most inappropriate times—while I was in bed with my lover, for instance. Really, I owe a lot to the tongue, that it never gave in and formed those sounds. It saved me, I don't know how many times, from what I couldn't bear to face again: the wall of that buttery moon.

If I blame the tongue for anything, I blame it for its independence. The tongue isn't anything like me. It isn't anything like my lover. After it had successfully boycotted certain words, it completely revolted, refusing to fulfill the simplest requests. Whenever the tongue did this, when it fell limp mid-sentence, my lover would stop what he was doing and wait for me to finish. What annoyed him more, though, was when, instead of finishing my sentence, I apologized for not finishing my sentence. When I apologized for apologizing for not finishing my sentence—well, it annoyed him that I thought it annoyed him. It annoyed me. But I couldn't control the tongue anymore.

"I'm not annoyed, I'm just trying to help," my lover would say. And I could tell that it disappointed him to discover that we were so different after all. He didn't have trouble finishing sentences. I wanted to tell him: Neither did I. But the tongue wouldn't let me. Then it was gone.

This is love, I tell myself. Love is silence.

Now everything is silence. The tongue floats in the jar. My lover lies on his back on the bed. I hug the wall.

Conjoined Twins Separated

As adolescents, they often said, whenever TV people came around with their questions, that one day they hoped to be a fashion designer and a mom. Actually, it was Crystal who'd provide this answer (Julie only ever stared at the camera), but to the interviewers, to everyone, it amounted to the same thing: the conjoined twins—of the dicephalic parapagus dibrachius type (meaning: two heads, one trunk, two arms), fused side-by-side and sharing a pelvis and set of legs—wanted to get pregnant.[1] In one documentary, this revelation was followed by a clip of the twins standing in a busy hallway of their middle school, Crystal waving her/their hand at someone off screen—a boy, it seemed, the camera having zoomed in on his chipped tooth and dimples. Cue voiceover (Mom): *Their private life is private. Do they have crushes on boys? Why wouldn't they?* After the short film aired, the anonymous boy reappeared to punch Julie in her spine (Crystal only felt their body lurching forward) and step around them and scrawl *Monster* in permanent marker across their lockers.[2]

---

[1] For a detailed illustration of the twins' insides, see the Discovery Channel's *One Body, Two Souls.*

[2] Conversely, were certain details of the twins' development in the womb slightly altered, the above might have appeared as follows:

> As children, they often said, whenever TV people came around with their questions, that one day they hoped to be a marine bi-ologist. Actually, it was Julie who'd provide this answer (Crystal

Not that being different ruled out all hope for the twins. On the internet, for instance, they found a picture of themselves in their cleavage-popping bathing suit (made by their seamstress to fit their wider torso), under which the caption read: Hot! It still counts as a threesome! Crystal squealed and laughed at this, but Julie felt her own armpit grow damp and thanked god her sister couldn't too. The idea of sex blazed through her mind—how it would work for them. Did Crystal, she wondered, already consider such things? Julie began to observe her sister in the mirror each morning as they took turns crimping or pinning back blond hair. Crystal's face was the more prominent, it being higher and better aligned with their body, but Julie was no less attractive for it, she didn't think. Would he, whoever he or *they* wound up being, kiss both or only one of them? This question obsessed her for years.[3]

After college, the twins moved out of their parents' house into a one-bedroom in their hometown and settled into a

---

only ever stared at the camera), but to the interviewers, to everyone, it amounted to the same thing: The conjoined twins—of the thoracopagus type (meaning: fused at the thorax and abdomen and sharing a heart), each with her own torso and sets of limbs—wished to probe great depths of brackish water. In the short film *I am Not a Freak*, this confession was followed by an animation of the twins in a conjoined scuba suit, strapped to their own oxygen tanks and synchronously kicking two sets of flippers, one on top of the other, past bright globs of coral, as if locked in an embrace. Ha-ha, the cartoonist seemed to say, Ha-ha. How silly.

[3] While this is certainly a plausible rendering of the lives of a set of dicephalic parapagus dibrachius twins, it by no means seeks to address the concerns of all types of conjoined twins. For instance, had Julie and Crystal been of the thoracopagus type and *not* shared a heart (refer to note 2), the text above might have read:

Then one day the twins' parents were contacted by a leading surgeon whose specialty it was to separate conjoined twins. Thus, Julie and Crystal underwent surgery on their sixteenth birthday.

career as an accountant. Soon they were receiving all manner of propositions from men whose Match.com profiles horrified them. Consequently, they remained a virgin.[4]

Neither twin worried overmuch about their maidenhood until their 29th birthday, when Crystal moaned: We might never have a baby! Then began explicit conversations—what they'd never before felt courageous enough to discuss. Masturbation had in their late teens—when they finally gave in to their urges—been mortifying, one girl waking to the other's fingers, silently sharing an orgasm, after which both pretended it hadn't happened, but now it seemed irrelevant. They skipped sex all together and went straight to the question of adoption. In truth, Crystal was far more eager to be a mother than Julie, who merely tolerated her twin's habit of clucking at and pawing their neighbors' babies, but their whole lives had been compromise, compromise, and Julie saw no point in ruining her sister's life. Not that her silence mattered. Crystal knew how she felt, just as Julie at this moment understood by her sister's neat crossing of their legs: *If I don't have a baby, Julie, I'll kill myself.* Aloud, Crystal offered: If you find Mr. Right, I'll do whatever you want if we have a baby. Thanks, Julie said, finding it difficult to imagine such a scenario, but I'm sure, she added, someone will let us adopt—if not, we'll sue. Then Crystal said: Maybe we've been too picky.

And so, they returned to Match.com. And soon went on date after date after gruesome date, after which, to Julie's relief, Crystal finally declared: I give up! Let's just steal a baby.

---

[4] But then again, if this story had begun, "As children," the previous passage above might have read (instead of what is posited in note 3):

> Then one day the twins' parents were contacted by a leading surgeon whose specialty it was to separate conjoined twins. Thus, Julie and Crystal underwent surgery on their fifth birthday.

That same night, however, Sherman, an ex-marine who'd brought Julie to Denny's the week before and then chatted mostly with her twin, called to ask Crystal bowling. Julie handed her the phone. We mean to get pregnant, her sister said. No nasty stuff. You can leave right after. —Ha, she said, he hung up. Coward. Then the phone rang again. Uh-huh, she said. No. No. She cocked her head to get a glimpse of her sister, the view all cheek and nostril. Great—lane three.

The next evening, Sherman greeted them with a shove toward the ball rack. You're late, he said. I hope it's not a habit.

It's my fault, Julie offered. Diarrhea, she added.

We didn't have diarrhea! Crystal jammed her fingers into a pink marbleized ball.

He plucked the ball from her hand. It's all right, sugar. We're having fun now, he said. And in half an hour, he was punching the air and yelling: That's what I'm talking about! That's how you play! Then he hollered for Crystal to record his strike.

Julie hissed: Abort Mission! Abort! And was not happy to hear: Well. It could be worse. He's not bad looking.[5]

Thus, the twins lost their virginity. The experience was unremarkable—disappointing. In less than a week, they got their period. Crystal thought it over for a while and then finally dialed up Sherman. Maybe he's sterile, Julie protested. *Sterile,*

---

[5] Consider replacing all the text thus far with the passages found in notes 2 & 3 and inserting this:

> After the twins were separated, they each recovered splendidly. Julie, always the more studious, stayed home more often now, reading and preparing for the SATs. After high school, she attended the University of Miami, earned a B.A., and then an M.S., and at last became a marine biologist in Southern Florida. Crystal became a realtor in their hometown and never left.

he barked, his voice replacing the ring tone. I don't know the meaning of the word sterile! And in forty minutes flat, he was at their apartment making a gallant effort to prove it. Right before he came, Crystal whooped such as Julie had never heard before; feeling nothing herself, she stifled her laughter.

When he finished, Sherman said, I thought—he narrowed his eyes at Julie, then Crystal—I thought it all worked the same down there.

It does, Crystal said. I mean, not all the time.

Hmm, he said and pulled up his jeans.

Anyway, he said, that one ought to do it. See you around, sugar.

When it *didn't* do it, he returned—again and again and again. But now he took to tossing his soiled undershirts on Julie's somber face, his hand tenderizing her breast while she tried not to feel as though she were being attacked. As soon as he left, she'd say: This has to stop.

Don't be selfish, Crystal said. We need him.

He's sweet, she added. The way he gazes into my eyes—

Is that so? Julie snapped. I wouldn't know.

You should be grateful he's so considerate, her sister said. He's not like the others, out for a thrill, some circus act. It's about me and him.[6]

Then began night after night of Sherman—Sherman telling anecdotes about war while stabbing the air with his switchblade (*Typical man!* Crystal's eye rolling would boast); Sherman setting off smoke detectors with his grilled cheeses

---

[6] For scenario 2B, refer to notes 2 & 4 and replace most of the above with the following:

> After the twins were separated, Crystal's half of their severed heart failed. She died at age five on her own operating table, never having woken to find her sister removed from her torso.

and baked ziti (*At least he tries*, Crystal's raised shoulder meant); Sherman snoring (*Like a puppy!* she'd say) on the roof of their apartment after an evening of wine and stargazing; Sherman displaying the portrait in his wallet of his dead "retarded" brother, as he, Sherman, weepy-eyed and distant (*So sensitive!*), fondled Crystal's breast; Sherman farting wetly, saying *Julie*, and wrinkling his nose in mock disgust until Crystal laughed an unfamiliar laugh. One that seemed with each passing month to resemble more and more Sherman's own honking guffaw. The two of them now in the habit of cupping a hand over the other's ear to whisper—whole conversations carried out in this manner on the couch, during which Sherman would slide a copy of *Vogue* or an empty pizza box between the girls' heads, a wall against Julie's eyes. As if that could block out the smooching, panting, unzipping, and finally Sherman himself.

[**Interpolate,** *verb* (used with object):

1) to introduce (something additional or extraneous) between other things or parts; interject; interpose; intercalate, 2) to alter (a text) by the insertion of new matter, especially deceptively or without authorization, 3) to insert (new or spurious matter) in this manner. (Dictionary.com)]

After a while, it became apparent that Sherman had moved in with them. The moving-in didn't happen in a single day but gradually as the year wore on, one article of clothing at a time, a fork at a time, a dish, a pot of stew he'd brought over and never taken back, hair clippers. It all made its way into cupboards and drawers and closets, the bathroom cabinet. Then one Sunday evening, he didn't go home. He was still there, in the bed, when the twins left for work the next morning, still there, on the couch, when they returned. Julie interrogated her sister: Is he living here now?

I have so much in common with him, Crystal said. More so, even, than with you.

Oh. Julie clutched her jaw as if a tooth ached.

[   ]⁷

The best part about being a conjoined twin, Crystal had once said in a TV interview, is that there is always someone to talk to and you're never alone.

But now Julie was always alone and there was never anyone to talk to. If she suggested visiting their parents, Crystal would roll her eyes for Sherman and mouth something like Baby or Maybe. Then the two of them would snigger and turn back to whatever it was they were doing, Julie the old chewing gum stuck to their carpet.

[   ]⁸

In the winter, because he was still on disability for PTSD and wanted to be helpful, Sherman drove the twins in their Honda to the office building in the center of town every morning and picked them up at five, sharp. Although Crystal

---

⁷ More than a decade had passed since Crystal awoke to find her twin lying in a separate hospital bed, and yet she still felt her sister attached to her like an amputee feels a phantom limb. While on the couch watching TV or driving to or from work, she would comment on this or that, as if Julie weren't thousands of miles away in Florida but still right there, attached to her and listening. This tendency of Crystal's disturbed others. Consequently, she remained alone.

⁸ No longer attached to her twin, Julie's little five-year-old body thrived. As she grew up, her parents told her: It isn't your fault. Her priest said: She died so that you could live. Her counselor: Let go of the guilt. Consequently, Julie wished she'd been the one to die.

and Julie had driven perfectly well for nearly fourteen years, he insisted upon acting as chauffeur. His sugar pie's life was a test and a chore, he said. And if he was anything in this bastard world, he was chivalrous. After all, didn't he used to walk his retarded brother to school every day? Didn't he punch his own father in the mouth for spitting chewing tobacco on and kicking Billy who was only moaning and banging his head against the floor, nothing to get angry about, it wasn't his fault he was a 'tard? So, yes, he'd drive his lady to work, and hell, to the grocery store and the bank, the post office, gynecologist, whatever she wanted. Would escort her to the passenger seat, buckle her in, and plant lips on her forehead. *Stay put*, he'd say and slam the door. Then get behind the wheel beside the ugly, sullen twin. He did all this because—well, because he was bored at home all day, okay, sure—but also because his sugar pie had years of hermitage to make up for and needed to be dragged out in the evening, sometimes during a snowstorm, goddamn it, for ice cream and movies and bowling.

Gosh, Crystal said from the passenger seat one day as Sherman went into the store to buy popcorn and beer. Isn't he a marvel? How did I ever survive without him?

Can you crack the window? Julie said, fanning her face. I'm dying in here.

Quit jostling us! Crystal said, turning sharply, her chin knocking into Julie's cheekbone.

Ouch!

Can't a body rest? Crystal wailed. Can't a body think?—without you. There. Interrupting.

She smashed her ponytail against the headrest, flinging Julie back with her, and gazed through the windshield at Sherman's tall figure at the register in the convenience store.

Julie eyed her sister's jaw, imagining the soft underside, near the throat.

If he ever left me, Crystal said, I'd kill myself.

And me, Julie said.

What?

—

What did you say?

Open the window. Bitch.

After lunch one day, a coworker stopped by the twins' cubicle and asked: Is that your boyfriend? She pointed to the framed photos arranged on the twins' desk like endangered coral reefs.

Crystal beamed. Of course, she said.

The woman looked at Crystal, then Julie, her eyes troubled with longing to ask something she dared not. Finally, she settled on: Why—aren't you two lucky? He's so tall!

I'm lucky, Crystal clarified. He's not living with Julie.

[   ]⁹

Lately, Julie found herself waking in the middle of the night to whispering. It was different from the daytime whispering. In the dark room, Crystal's frantic Shh! would strangle Sherman's dull rumble, and then her head would turn gently on the pillow: Julie? Are you awake?

It was no use pretending.

---

⁹ Over the years, the twins developed the habit of calling each other every few months to give updates on their lives. Crystal's accounts of herself as a lonely realtor hardly ever varied. Julie's updates brimmed with aquatic adventures and land romances. Then one phone call she announced that she was getting married. Would Crystal be a bridesmaid? She already had a maid of honor.

You snoop, Crystal would say. I know you're faking. Can't I ever have any privacy?

Tell her, honey. She deserves to know.

Tell me what? Julie said.

No!

Soon, Julie noticed another strange thing. Every time she typed a word beginning with a *c* into the Google search engine, *conjoined twins* popped up in the autofill. The first time it happened, Crystal grew tense. I guess, Julie said, you've been educating yourself, huh, Sherman?

He turned from the TV. What the hell is she talking about? he said. But Crystal stared at the computer screen, unhearing. She swallowed.

Julie dropped the subject. Let's go to the bathroom.

I don't have to go.

Yes, you do.

No. I don't. Her upper lip quivered.

Julie had long ago lost the ability to read her sister. She'd come to feel as if a stranger's head and arm had been transplanted onto her body. Before Sherman, she and Crystal had navigated the world like a single entity, their minds unconsciously collaborating to perform daily tasks like showering or cooking or driving. Now even their gait was awkward. Julie, no longer able to anticipate her sister's next move, often felt as if she were being dragged along like dead weight.

[   ]¹⁰

---

¹⁰ After many years of counseling, Julie was finally able to say aloud: No one blames me. But secretly she continued to feel guilty. At age thirty, she would often return from her receptionist job at the spa in town and flop onto the couch to disappear into the documentary *I Am Not a Freak*. For a few minutes, Crystal's freckles would be resurrected,

In the spring, Julie received a wedding invitation in the mail. Her name was written in Sherman's childish hand on the outside of the envelope. *July 4*, the card inside read. Independence Day.

Why are you crying? Crystal demanded. Shouldn't you be happy?

Then Julie said: Why are *you* crying?

The following week, the letters *s-e* became *separation surgery*. Julie went cold. She let her hand fall from the mouse and stared at the computer screen.

Goddamn him, Crystal mumbled.

What—what. Julie's tongue hobbled like a clubfoot. What's going on?

Nothing! Crystal burst into tears. They can do nothing for us! Nothing!

Ah hell, Sherman said and got off the couch. I said I'd still marry you, didn't I? It's you who's making a stink. He stalked to the bathroom and slammed the door.

Julie said, But.

Never mind. Crystal sniveled. If we went through with it, we'd both die. Then she said bitterly: Your chances of survival are slightly higher.

After that, Julie refused Crystal's attempts to help fix her hair and soon gave up washing it. In the wedding pictures that lined the walls of their cubicle, you couldn't tell. A pink scarf had been tactfully wrapped around her head. It was, after all, not her wedding. Even still, Crystal had the

---

her five-year-old voice fill the dark room. The best part, she'd say into the camera, is that there is always someone to talk to and you are never alone.

morning of the ceremony speared her sister's lips with a tube of red gloss, saying, exasperated:

Don't you want to be pretty?

Julie slapped her sister's hand away.

During the ceremony, flashes of light penetrated the pink silk. She'd imagined herself to be like a closed tulip balanced on the shoulder of the striking blond in virgin white.

Now she knew better. Photographs didn't lie.

[   ]11

Then it was winter again. Then it was spring. Then summer hit. Then Crystal, now a desperate thirty-two, once more took up the subject of her closing window of motherhood.

It was not a topic Sherman favored. When his wife cornered him and demanded he make her a baby, he'd argue: But what about her? And nod at the extra head on her shoulder.

She's got nothing to do with it.

What will the kid call her?

I told you. She's got nothing to do with it.

Then Julie was no longer Julie but a seahorse floating in a tank of brackish water. Her black eyes were pressed up against the scummy glass, trained on the tall man jabbing his finger at the two-headed monster, his voice a broken

---

11 Crystal, a lonely spinster at thirty, envied her twin's engagement and resented only being one of eight bridesmaids. At the wedding hall, she was led into a back room where Julie, whom she hadn't seen in years, sat in front of a vanity mirror, pinning blond hair into a bun. Darling! Julie breathed. Her eyes fixed on the glass. She turned in her chair. But I hardly recognized you! Then she stood, fists clamped to her billowing skirt. And Crystal saw it: a perfect bowling ball above the waist, right where she once lived.

gurgle on the surface above. Then the monster said: You're killing me! I wish I could die! And Julie came crashing out of the tank and onto the floor.

Julie grew corpulent and debilitated by guilt. She aged quickly and died of heart failure.

Julie married an ex-marine named Sherman. A few months later, they had twins.

Oh, Work!

Maybe I was lonely—bored. Maybe Jack was bored too. I remember thinking when he asked me out: Why not. Better him, better anyone, than another night alone with these fingers. Maybe I was horny. (That's what happens, they say, in a woman's late twenties: sex on the brain.)

Our first date, after finishing a few cans of Sapporo, Jack threw me over his shoulder in the middle of the Japanese restaurant and started smacking my ass. That, he later told me, was how he seduced the last girl. It was how he seduced me. Up until that point in the evening, I'd been eyeing my fingers, sending them telepathic messages: *I'll never cheat on you again, I'm sorry, I was stupid.* But the instant my ass was bouncing six feet up in the air, Jack's face pressed against my thigh, I forgot all about the fingers.

Now I wish I'd been more faithful.

Dating Jack was like dating my weirdest dreams. While I was with him that year, I didn't know why I did most of what I did. What I did know was: I wasn't bored anymore. Most of the time, I wasn't even horny.

When I met him, we were both living in Brooklyn. I was working some crummy temp job, he an art-handling gig. Eventually, I don't remember how it happened, he moved in with me. A month later, my roommate moved out. Before leaving, she said: "You've really changed." And I took her to mean: *You've grown too big for me.*

With her gone, the place felt less cluttered. We felt less cluttered. We stopped doing stuff, stopped buying toilet paper. "What's the sense in that," Jack said, "with all these trees around?" And I guess I didn't know: What *was* the sense in toilet paper? And so, now, instead of rolls of white, we had fistfuls of maple leaves stockpiled on the floor beside the bowl. After only a few days, the leaves would start to crumble mid-wipe, but I never complained.

When the economy turned to shit, and I lost my job and went on unemployment, Jack pouted: "That's not fair. I want to get paid to do nothing too." And within the week, having gotten himself fired from his job, he was taking his coffee out onto the fire escape, and calling to me, every now and again—"Look at those chumps! Rushing to get to work on time! Their life isn't their own!"—while diligently filling out unemployment paperwork in his bathrobe.

After that, Keep-from-Growing-Bored became priority number one. No idea was too strange too crazy too stupid to entertain.

Once, we found a broken wheelchair in a dumpster and brought it back home, where we took turns sitting in it like vegetables, our skulls duct-taped to the headrest, drool dripping from our lopsided mouths. Then Jack got a brilliant idea, and we went to Coney Island with it (the idea), carrying the wobbly wheelchair down several flights of stairs and onto the D train. It was summer then, and Jack in his bathrobe and I in my nurse's uniform (a karate pants and muumuu combo), dragging a rusty wheelchair from one end of the car to the other, drew more attention from the weekend beachgoers than we'd expected.

On the boardwalk, Jack got into the wheelchair, as planned, and I, in my heavy getup, began to sweat profusely (*not* as planned).

"Did you set it, yet?" Jack asked.

I checked my watch: "Yes. We have five minutes."

The sun was directly overhead, the beach packed with towels, umbrellas, sunbathers. It felt, for a moment, as if I might suffocate, and I considered abandoning the mission.

"Well, then," he said, taping his forehead to the chair. "We'd better get started," and before I could change my mind, I pushed him out onto the sand.

The wheels sank immediately. "You're too heavy," I said, struggling with all my weight to push him forward. "Maybe you should get out."

"No, no," he whispered. "People are watching."

It was true: a family of overweight sunbathers had already turned their heads toward us, their mouths partly open.

So, the mission had begun. I, instant Nurse, started tending to my paralytic patient. I took off his slippers and rolled up his pajamas and stretched his legs out in the sun. I squirted a bottle of water in his face to cool him off and then combed back his wet hair. I sat in the sand beside him and took in the view of colorful bathing suits and towels and choppy ocean. My eyes met those of our chubby onlookers, and I smiled brightly: "Nice day, huh!"

No one returned the smile.

Then the alarm on my wrist went off, and I, very pointedly, brought the time to my face before thumbing the stop button. I stood up, brushing the sand off my hands. "Okay, Mister," I announced, loud enough for our family. "It's time, your favorite part of the day."

And like a competent professional, ever ready to meet her patient's needs, I opened Jack's bathrobe and reached in through the hole in his pajamas and pulled out his penis. It was limp and cold and gray. But in my hand, it began to twitch, and as I worked it into stiffness, very mechanically, masterfully, you might say, I looked over at the family of fatsoes, and sigh-smiled, as if to say, Oh *work*! What can you do?

A look of horror had settled on their faces. And then suddenly they were packing up their belongings and saying things like: "My God." "What *freaks*." "Don't look at that, kids!"

We watched them scurrying off, Jack and I, his penis going soft in my hand. And we laughed, and we laughed, and we thought: Today we were not bored.

The Lonely Planet

Buffalo is quicksand. Ask Chuck's family, ask their friends. Ask anybody. Go into one of the pubs and bars and pubs and more pubs. On a Tuesday or Monday, go in, ask. None of them have ever liked it here, yet, after a while, they were stuck, couldn't get out. That's Buffalo. Chuck has never lived anywhere else. He's never been out of the country—unless you count, as most of his relatives do, his crossing the bridge to see Niagara Falls. But Chuck is a college graduate now. He won't end up like them. He has a plan.

"Thailand?" his uncle squawks at the graduation party. "What the hell do you want to go to that gook country for?" The plan: choose country (the farther from here, the better); travel to country (stranger, the better). Of all the destinations—Mexico, France, Egypt, Australia, Russia—Chuck has tested out on his guests this afternoon, none has come close to achieving this level of astonishment. "Sherry!" his uncle yells from the above-ground pool where he stands in boxer shorts, his gut like the rump of a wading hog. "You'd better get your scrawny ass over here! The communications major has something to share."

A puff of blond curls appears below. "What the hell do you want, Barry?"

"Ask your son"—pointing his koozied can at the boy—"where he plans to spend his summer."

"Is that a cigarette? Barry, did you give him that?" She yanks off a high heel, slaps it against the aluminum paneling at Chuck's back. "You're a smoker now, huh?"

He looks at her. Samples the word on his dull tongue, "Thailand." Imagines himself in a conical hat, bending over a rice paddy. He says it again louder. "What do you think of that, Ma?"

"You're a damned fool, that's what she thinks!"

"What do I care?" She jams her foot back into the pump. "You'll be dead soon, anyway, smoker."

So it is decided. A round-trip ticket purchased. Farewells made. And then: the flight. Not until Chuck is on the plane, lifting off the tarmac—only his second time flying (the first being his trip to Missoula for his Dad's funeral eight years ago)—not until then, as the ground drops away and his back presses into the seat, does it sink in: in twenty-eight hours, he'll be in Bangkok. . . . And then what? He tries to picture himself there, wandering out of the airport and finding his way to a hostel. But he sees only darkness. He turns to the window, searches the ground for the airport parking lot and his mom's pickup truck, its rust lost in the distance, a glaring blinding thing—that's how he pictures *that*, the sight of her truck from the sky. How it might have looked, if the aircraft's shadow weren't already gliding over the permed heads of trees. An image floats to the surface of his mind, something he's seen in his travel guide: rows of bald teenage boys in neon-orange robes kneeling before a gold Buddha, their copper hands clasped in prayer. Maybe, he thinks, he should have put more thought into the plan.

From Tokyo to Bangkok, the last leg of his flight, Chuck meets Alex, a Brit. It's the first time he's ever spoken to someone with an English accent. "It's my gap year," the Briton explains. Chuck blinks, and the young man continues: "I figure I'll stay as long as my money holds out. I don't have a return ticket. How long are you traveling?"

Chuck boasts, "Five weeks."

"Right," the Brit says absently, "just for a holiday." He returns to his book, turns a page, then, brightening: "I've always wanted to go to New York. Is it as dangerous as they say?"

"Oh," Chuck fumbles, realizing that the Brit has confused the state with the city. "Yes." Ashamed to admit that he's never stepped foot on the island. "Very."

Later, as they wait at the baggage carousel for their rucksacks, the Brit suggests they share a taxi, "To save money, and all that," since they both, no doubt, have the same destination: Khao San Road.

In this way, Chuck finds himself, at last, in Thailand. Drinking Singha beer and eating pizza in the restaurant of a popular hostel, opposite his new friend, the Brit. At the table with them are a Dutch couple and a German, the occupants of the other beds in their dorm. Already, Chuck hears himself lecturing people back home: "Oh, the Dutch! Ah...Germans! Those British...!" Inwardly he glows with satisfaction. Arriving in Thailand, he realizes, is a bit like being admitted into Harvard (or anyway how a professor of his once described it): getting in is a son of a bitch, but once there, it's next to impossible to fail. That, the prof said, is Harvard's most guarded secret. Of course, stuck as he was at Buff State, the old man was probably just embittered. And, aside from some anxiety on the plane, Chuck wasn't particularly intimidated by the idea of exploring Asia. Nonetheless, he likes the comparison. The folks back home, at any rate, will certainly be impressed by his exotic stories and pictures—which reminds him… He takes out his camera, snaps a couple photos of his new friends. Twenty feet past their table in the open restaurant, auto rickshaws—tuk-tuks, the German called them—buzz between the passersby in the pedestrian road, the drivers beeping at those with large backpacks while shouting "You!" "Where you want to go?" "Hey!" "I bring you!" It's midnight. Humid. Tourists—many with dreadlocks, some in need of a shower—scurry from street vendor to street vendor; clutter the food stalls and carts; sit cross-legged on the sidewalk; pass in and out of entrances under flashing lights. Only a couple of hours ago, Chuck had stared at a stall door in the airport bathroom, haunted by the sense of his never having left Buffalo. Now he's aware of someone speaking to him. New York, the voice says.

It's the German. "What's your story, New York? How long are you traveling?"

Chuck glances at the Brit and, seeing him distracted with the Dutch couple, hazards: "Whenever my savings run out. I don't have a return ticket."

The German nods.

Then the Dutch woman, apparently listening, says, "Gosh, I envy you guys!" She slides her chair closer. "Are you and Alex traveling together, then?"

"So far, yes."

"We could only get a month off ourselves," she says. "I thought that'd be plenty of time, but I see now it's not. The other day, we met a Canadian who's been traveling since last July. Came up from Australia, picking fruit along the way, and is heading to India. Can you imagine?"

"I might teach English here," Chuck says, recalling the ad he saw tacked to the hostel's bulletin board earlier tonight, "stay even longer." The thought of one day beginning his sentences with *Yes, but when I worked in Thailand* thrills him.

"You don't," the German asks, "intend to teach in Bangkok, I hope?"

"It is a bit dodgy, isn't it," the Brit says. "All I've seen so far are a bunch of white faces."

"The city's a hub," the German agrees. "I fly back to Berlin tomorrow." He stamps the last slice of pizza with his empty Singha bottle. "Do yourselves a favor. See the temples, then leave. Don't get sucked in. One day, maybe two is all you really need."

"What about the islands?" the Brit asks.

"They're lovely," the Dutch woman says, and then checks herself. "If you like that sort of thing." To her boyfriend, she says, "It was a circus, right? Drag queens, drunks, kids." She takes a pull off her cigarette. "Koh Samui and Koh Phi Phi, I mean. Phuket, I've heard, is worse."

"I'll tell you what's worse," the German says. "All those damn treks being run through hill-tribe villages. It's a racket. You and eighteen *farangs* tramping through the jungle, stopping every five minutes to let some moron take a photo of a colorful bug"—Chuck slides his camera into his pants pocket—"then taking over a village for a night to ogle the natives in their homes. *Authentic experience*, my ass! More like having an overnight pass to the zoo."

"Shit," the Dutch woman's boyfriend says, "that's where we're headed next."

The Brit wonders aloud, "Is nowhere unspoiled?" and the travelers at the table fall silent. Outside, in the road: the same chaotic pulse. Now bereft of its allure. This isn't really Thailand, Chuck thinks, his spirits sagging. It's an amusement park—exciting, different, but not *authentic*.

The Dutch man turns to the German. "Where did you travel while you were here?"

"Let's see," he says and ticks off on his fingers: "Chiang Mai. Then into Laos: Luang Prabang. I crossed over into Vietnam, worked my way down from Hanoi to Saigon—they still call it that—and came back through Cambodia. You *must* see the sun rise over Angkor Wat, all of you. It'll change your life."

Chuck perks up. "How long does it take to do all that?"

"Oh. Well." He scratches his neck. "It depends on the person, I'd say."

"But how much time did you spend here?"

"Not nearly enough."

"Yes, but—"

"I'm guessing," the Brit cuts in, "it takes a lot longer than five weeks, New York."

"What happens in five weeks?" the Dutch woman asks. She picks up her beer and glances at her boyfriend. Follows his gaze. "God," she says, "that one's younger than my baby sister!"

They turn to look. In a corner of the restaurant, near the hostel's lobby, a striking Thai girl in jeans and halter top raises a bottle to her lips. At the table with her, a pudgy, pink-faced man talks on his phone, his bald, pale crown gleaming. He cups the mouthpiece with a palm and leans forward to say something. She collects her long black hair in a pile over a shoulder, smiles.

"Predator," the Dutch woman says.

Over the next eight days, Chuck visits the Grand Palace, Wat Traimit, Wat Benjabophit, Wat Pho. He listens to monks chanting in the dazzling porcelain and marble temples, drops coins into bowls along the base of the reclining Buddha, its gold body like an entombed cargo ship. He samples exotic fruit from the world's largest open-air market, places bets at Muay Thai kickboxing matches, cringes at the snake farm as men with amputated fingers pretend to throw cobras and mambas at the bleachers. He rides water taxis up and down the river, hails tuk-tuks, takes the Skytrain. He learns to shower the sweat off his body twice a day, how to say hello (*sa-wa-dee-kraup*), what *farang* means (foreigner). He watches *The Beach* twice, once at the restaurant in his hostel, another time at a bar down the road, and is stirred by it, wonders if his German friend saw the film. He eats Pad Thai in a dinner theatre while women in glittering Eiffel-Tower-shaped crowns seduce him on stage with their double-jointed fingers. He gets lonely. Every place he visits is swamped by tourists. He scans their faces, hoping to recognize one, find his Brit or the Dutch couple. A futile habit, he knows. By now they might be in Laos or Cambodia. Not stuck here like a fool, a coward. If only they didn't disappear that first morning, invited him along—wherever they were going.

Navigating Bangkok has been painless, what with his hostel arranging tours and his travel guide being so thorough. Any idiot, he thinks, could travel here. He suspects that other places in Thailand will be just as accommodating. Yet he can't seem to bring himself to leave the capital, despite his alarm at the loss of precious time. It's ironic, he thinks, how he could board a plane to a distant exotic land, and then, once here, be struck by such inertia.

On the ninth day, having run out of things to do, he lets a tuk-tuk driver take him on a special tour of the "unknown wonders of the city," during which he is shown a small temple down the street, and then bullied into entering the shops of a tailor and a jeweler and a travel agency. In this last, Chuck sits beside a desk and stares at the photographs tacked to the wall behind the pretty travel agent. "Very authentic," she assures him, pointing at a thatched-roof hut on stilts. "You sleep first night at campsite in jungle. Second night, stay in Karen village"—she indicates another picture: a barefoot woman squatting on the dirt floor of a smoke-filled room and stirring a pot of food above open flames—"like this. You take plenty photo." Then she taps the map displayed before him under the glass desktop and traces her finger from Bangkok up to Chiang Mai. "Ten hours on train. They pick you up at station, bring you to guesthouse. You start trek next day, only two-hour drive. But first you ride elephant and take bamboo raft down river. See?" She thumbs the wall again. Pale faces smile back at him from atop dusty elephants and wide rafts sliding over brown water. "We take care, all of it. You pay cheap."

Chuck imagines how he'd look on the back of an elephant: like Harrison Ford in *The Temple of Doom*. Then he remembers the German, what he'd said about the treks up north, and the image fades. "Thanks," he says, rising to join the tuk-tuk driver outside, "but I shouldn't."

"Where you go next? You fly home?"

"No. I don't know." He feels stupid. His eyes settle on a map. "Laos? I mean, yes. Laos."

"Oh! Beautiful place! You have visa?"

He checks the door. The driver is leaning against the glass, rubbing his eyes. "Well…no."

"We get you one, no problem. It take only one day." She smiles. "How you get there?"

"Um, I—I don't know."

"Fine, no problem, we help that too." She nods her head at the chair. "Please. Sit."

"Look, miss—"

"You look." She taps her map again. "You take train to Chiang Mai, stay one night at guesthouse. They drive you next day to border crossing where you get on slow boat. Two days on Mekong River—very beautiful!" She opens a drawer and hands him a photo. In it, a wooden boat shaped like a lazy, thin smile glides over red-ochre water in front of a broccoli-studded limestone cliff. On the shore of the tiny island, barely perceptible in the picture, is a single hut.

"Who lives there?" Chuck asks, forgetting himself.

"You go to Luang Prabang." She takes back the photo. "That just view on way."

"And it's all taken care of?" he says, his mind lingering on the isolated hut. Did the German, he wonders, go there, see that? "I don't have to figure anything out?"

"We take care, all of it: transportation, visa, accommodations." She opens another drawer, pulls out a form. "When you come back? We take care that, too."

He sinks back onto the chair. "How long do most people stay?"

"You can do it quick or stay long time, up to you."

"Maybe," he says, hesitant, "I'd like to decide later?"

She looks at the door. The driver points at his watch. "Sure, sure," she says, "you decide later, no problem. We need passport and deposit. You pick up visa and tickets in three days."

"I thought you said it only takes one day?"

"Consulate closed Sunday. And it too late today."

On the day of his departure, Chuck is grateful for the return of his passport. This makes him feel guilty—that he ever doubted the agent. Then he wonders if he ought to feel guilty, if his distrust wasn't merely a sign of prudence. After which thought, he learns that he is to take a night train to Chiang Mai. "You save money on accommodation," the travel agent explains, "save daylight for sightseeing." He thanks her and collects his tickets, pleased with his own good judgment in allowing this woman to see to it all.

But hours later, after rolling out his sleeping bag on the bunk above his seat, then climbing up into the cubby and sliding the curtain shut, he curses that damn woman. Since at least ten o'clock, when he saw the first man disappear into his bunk, he had wanted badly to lie down like this, curled up and hidden, but couldn't bring himself to stand and be gawked at again. Instead, he glared at the reflections in the black window: the wide cheekbones of a Thai woman asleep in her seat; the old monk across the aisle whose bright robes lit the glass like dawn; the baseball-capped man, in the next seat up, quietly scratching his lap. In the center of them all, Chuck's own stupid face: sunburnt, bags under his eyes. Now, at half past midnight, he finally closes them—and instantly feels himself hurtling through darkness, a moth sucked into a vacuum-cleaner tube and traveling to the belly of dust and fever. He tries to blot out this sensation, fixes on the image of the white limestone cliff rising from the small hut below.

In the morning, he wakes to the sound of fork on plate. He pulls the curtain back an inch and sees the shiny head of the monk bending over fried eggs and toast. The attendant wheels her coffee station up to the monk, asks him something and, when he nods, nudges the baseball-capped man and hands him the cup of coffee. He turns around and passes it to the monk. Chuck wonders at this, and then the monk is staring back at him, the coffee's steam rising into his aged face. "Good morning," the monk says.

Chuck yanks the curtain shut. Then opens it and clambers down the ladder, feeling dumb. He sits in his seat, opens the shade, and gasps. A green as brilliant as a picture-book jungle, its banana trees like dinosaur-sized feather dusters, streams past the window. "Holy!" he says and turns to the aisle. But no one is there—just the monk, frowning at his coffee, his index finger and thumb fishing in the cup.

"You're late," a Thai man greets him on the platform. Chuck follows him through the station and out into the parking lot. A van door slides open, and he feels his rucksack being lifted off his shoulders—then he's shoved inside, and the door is slammed shut. "He'd better be the last one," someone mutters. Chuck lifts his head to find a group of tourists buckled into their seats. "Might as well get comfy down there, mate," a man behind him says. "They've overbooked this thing."

Chuck raises his voice to the driver. "How far are we from the guesthouse?"

"What guesthouse?" the Thai man says, starting the engine. "We're going to the border."

"But I have accommodations. They were arranged for me. I already paid."

"You got the night train," he says. "No need to stay in Chiang Mai." He pulls into traffic, speeds up. "If we dropped you off, everyone else would miss their boat."

"But—"

A hand drops onto his shoulder and grips it tightly. "Tough luck, mate."

By the time they reach Chiang Kong and hop out at immigration, Chuck's knees ache, and he's in a foul mood. He says nothing to the tourists waiting with him to get their passports stamped. On the ferry to Laos, he sits on a bench inside, glaring at the *farangs* out on the deck snapping pictures of the Mekong.

"Are you getting the slow boat?" a dark-haired girl, fourteen at most, asks. She sips orange liquid from a straw in a plastic bag. The real thing, he thinks: a native. Talking to him.

He winks at her. "That's right." And immediately feels old, awkward. "Are you?"

"It already left." She flicks a thick braid off her chest. "You'll have to stay in Huay Xai."

"Are you sure?" He studies her warm round face. Is she lying? "We were rushed here."

"It always leaves at noon." Her plump lips close around the straw as she studies him. She smiles. "Are you a movie star?"

"Oh. Ha." He fidgets with a strap on his bag. "Do you watch a lot of American movies? Your English is very good." She shrugs, her dark eyes bright. "What if," he says, "I am famous?"

"Bloody hell!" a voice behind him says. "First I run into that Dutch couple in Chiang Mai, and now here you are." The Brit sits down. "Cute kid. Does she speak any English? Hey kid, where's your mum? Don't you know you can't trust a New Yorker?"

She makes a face and scoots away on the bench.

Chuck growls, "What the fuck?"

"Well, it's nice to see you too." He follows Chuck's gaze to the girl. "Oh, I get it," he sneers. "You've got the fever, New York. You cunt! You're positively sick with it."

Chuck eyes him suspiciously. "What are you trying to pull? I feel fine."

"I'll bet!" He slaps Chuck on the back. "*Fine*, ha!"

And just like that, Chuck is no longer alone. On the slow boat the next day, he asks the Brit about the Dutch couple. "If I were them," his friend concludes, "I'd leave my job. Can you imagine missing this?" He positions his elbow on the corner of a tarp to keep it from flapping open. Already his shirt is half soaked with rain. He shifts on the bench. "My ass is numb!"

An older woman turns. "Language. You're representing your country, an ambassador."

"My god, lady," the Brit says. "This is no place to stop taking your meds."

Her face blanches. "Could you at least put out your cigarette?" She gives a weak cough, a flabby fist cupping her thin lips. "Where I come from—"

"What cigarette?" he challenges. "Where *I* come from, people have something called manners. Do you mind?" He turns to Chuck. "As—I—was—saying." He waits for her to turn around. "Right: our Dutch couple. They decided to do that trek, after all. Do you remember? They told us they were going? Lady!" he barks at the woman bent across the aisle, whispering. "Don't go peddling your poison! They all know your ass is sore." He takes a drag and blows it at her empty backrest.

"*Americans*," Chuck says, and is instantly pleased with himself. The Brit may have changed since Chuck last saw him, but so has he. He's practically a new man. Two weeks here have done that.

"Definitely American," the Brit agrees.

"So," Chuck says, unsure how to proceed. "What happened on the trek?"

"They said it was beastly. An elephant track circling the inside of a village. Half-naked kids with pot bellies glaring up at them. Some threw pebbles, I understand. Hit the elephants."

"Glad I skipped that!"

"Goddamn tourists," the Brit says, "they ruin everything."

"*Tourists!*" Chuck agrees.

The Brit frowns: "You're a bit of a dolt, aren't you?"

"Ho, shit!" a guy behind them says. "She's topless."

"What do you mean, 'dolt'?"

The Brit laughs and peels back the tarp. "Not bad," he says. "Have a look." Chuck glares at him. "You don't want a peek?" the Brit says. "She reminds me of your girl with the braid."

"Whatever," Chuck snorts. He crosses his arms, then: "What's she doing?"

"Laundry, I think."

Chuck leans across the Brit's lap, sticks his head out the window. A flash of golden brown: a bare arm and shoulder blade. "Damn! We already passed her."

"Cunt."

When the boat finally docks at a village along the Mekong, the Brit lifts the tarp and hops out in waist-deep water. Chuck watches him trudge to shore as the Laotians piling backpacks on the muddy bank stop their work to yell at the white figure rising out of the murky water. The Brit ignores them, scoops up his rucksack, and heads up the hill to the guesthouse.

Chuck spots him that night dining on the deck with a few tourists. He leaves the bar, heads over to their table. "Another day on that crap boat!" the Brit is saying, his fist strangling a Beerlao. "I doubt I'll survive it."

"Makes you wish you took the fast boat, aye?"

"Feck," a woman says, "my arse is killing me."

"It was packed to the gills," Chuck slurs, slinking into a chair, "a bunch of dumb white faces." He stamps his beer into the melted wax on the table, then raises the bottle to his lips. His eyes focus on its end—a leaf of some sort stuck there, hanging. No: a moth.

"Are you pissed?"

Chuck looks up.

The Brit's face is hostile. "Or are you completely daft?"

"Sorry?"

"Forget it," the woman says. "He's right. Look around you. It's shite. Horny tourists—"

"How is everything?" A hand reaches past Chuck's arm, collecting empty bottles. "Can I get you anything else?" Chuck hiccups. "Another round!" he says. The girl's hand disappears.

"Oops." The woman at the table titters. "Do you think she heard me?"

But the Brit is still scowling at Chuck, who pretends not to notice. His eyes follow the waitresses flitting from table to table. Earlier this evening he was surprised to discover that behind the hostel there was nothing but a mud path, along which stood a dozen wood huts. The store was just a window cut out of a shed, its products—snacks and toiletries—displayed on a platform. That was it. No roads. No bikes. Nothing. Imagine, he thinks now, if he were stuck here. What kind of life would that be? He tries to envision himself waking in a single-room hut and going to the outhouse, dipping a plastic bowl into a basin of water and emptying it into the porcelain hole in the ground to flush his morning crap. He photographed a toilet like that at immigration in Huay Xai. Just because the guesthouse has porcelain thrones doesn't mean the waitresses get to wipe their privates over a Western bowl at home. The thought excites him. He considers broaching the topic, but how? "There's no plumbing in this village," he says, "is there? I mean, apart from the guesthouse. These girls probably have to squat over an open pit."

"What are you getting at, New York?"

"This is nothing!" another man says. "Up north, where we're coming from, we slept in huts, used candles at night. The villagers didn't have ice, had never seen a digital camera."

"We were basically the only ones there," his friend chimes in, "aside from a German."

The Brit leans forward. "How did you get there?"

"*That's* nothing," the woman says. "A guy I met told me about a friend of his who hired his own boat and went as far north as he could in Laos. The natives ran from him, called him a ghost. They'd never seen a white person before. Never mind a camera."

The Brit says, "He hired his own boat?"

"Me," she continues, opening a pack of cigarettes, "I'd rather leave them alone. Let them go on existing without knowledge of the outside world. Technology isn't doing us any good."

"Oh, bullocks, that's just selfish idealism."

"Selfish! *Look* at these blokes. The damage they've already—"

"Five Beerlaos," the waitress announces to the table.

Chuck catches her attention, winks. "Do you have plumbing?—at home?"

She plunks the bottles on the table, one by one. "Your tab is still running at the bar," she answers. "Should I add this to it?"

"What about toilet paper? Or do you use your fingers? Your English is impeccable." He fishes out his wallet. "Wait! Come back! I'm gonna give it to you."

"You *are* pissed."

"See what I *mean?*"

"Do I remind you guys of anyone? A movie star?"

"Someone put this cunt to bed."

"Let's ask the waitress. Maybe she'll recognize me. Hey. Wait. Hey."

"Eejit."

"Follow me and I'll topple you, New York."

He wakes to a crowing rooster. His sheet soaked in sweat. For a moment, he can't remember where he is or why the bed is canopied in dark netting. Mosquito net. He pushes his head against the nylon, forcing his way out, then finds the hole and tumbles to the floor. He staggers to the bathroom, lifts the toilet seat, and holds himself while gazing out the window at the pink sky. His mouth is dry, his head screaming. Down below on the shore, a group of Laotians huddle around a tall blond—the Brit. One man grabs the Brit's hand and pulls him toward a speedboat. Another man slaps the hand away and wraps his own around the Brit's arm, points at a different boat. The Brit nods, hands over his rucksack, and follows him. The Laotians scatter.

Chuck rushes back to his room. He dresses quickly, stuffs his belongings into his backpack. Then thinks: What am I doing? He plops onto the bed. He has, he calculates, at least two hours before the boat leaves for Luang Prabang. He could go down to the restaurant, check things out. Walk around the village. Yes, he thinks, that's more sensible. Yes. Why rush off? Who cares where the Brit's going. I'll be fine. Yes. There. It's decided. He gets up, the bag still in his arms, and heads to the restaurant's deck.

"You too?" a waiter says. "Breakfast doesn't start until seven."

"Are you the only server here?"

The man folds his arms. "Why?"

"Never mind."

Chuck wanders out of the restaurant feeling lost, alone. Decides to head to the shore, maybe say goodbye to the Brit. But halfway down the hill, he veers off the path and walks through the woods to the water. He's thirsty. Hot. Maybe he'll roll up his pants, wade in the river. Branches scratch his arms and face, get caught on his backpack. Sucking mud clings to his sneakers. He steps out into the clearing, drops his bag in the sand. And then he sees her, standing waist-deep in the brown water: a bare-chested girl rolling a soapy garment over the flat surface of a submerged boulder. "Good morning," she says.

"Oh." He takes a step back. "Hi."

She nods and returns to her washing. A basket of laundry sits on a dry corner of the stone. On another corner, she kneads the sudsy garment like dough. He studies her: Is she the waitress? Her black hair is wet and twisted over one shoulder. Her breasts copper, plump. He feels himself growing hard.

"Mind if I sit here?"

She dips the cloth in the water and rings it out, shrugs. Her eyes still lowered.

"Thanks," he says and plants his butt in the sand. "Beautiful here," he adds. Then he recalls the photo the travel agent showed him, the isolated hut. Maybe this girl lives in something like that, he thinks. Maybe, if I offer her some money, she'll show it to me. An engine starts on the water nearby. The girl doesn't stir. Soon a speedboat comes into view. As it blazes past them, Chuck sees the Brit's hand go up, sees his big-toothed grin. The girl picks a dry shirt out of the basket, her eyes trained on the boulder. Then the Brit is gone. Chuck unzips his pants, says, "I'm from Buffalo." She rubs soap on the shirt, lathers it.

Pucka! Pucka! Pucka!

I lost my boyfriend to a gorilla named Malika. She beat her chest at him, and that was that: he forgot me entirely. People ask me all the time now, Where's Roger? and I say: the zoo. What? they spit back, confused. Now? (In our world—that is, the world Roger once inhabited with me, academia—people don't, as a rule, take up residence at the zoo.) That's where he is, I say and pick at the Miller label on my warm bottle. The gorilla exhibit.

Usually they titter at this, and then scan the bar for an escape. If we're outdoors, enjoying the summer night, one of them might look up at the orange sky and point to a star that none of us can see. Their brains hum all the while with interpretation: gorilla, the zoo. Roger. What they must take for metaphor. This much seems clear to everyone: he and I are not in a good place.

One of these days one of these colleagues of ours is going to take my answer literally, sneak into the zoo, and call my bluff. Roger does not spend his nights pacing the fence that separates him from the manmade ravine that separates him from his love. Every evening at six o'clock, sharp—the staff is careful not to let him linger—a man in a golf cart herds him toward the exit. But the next morning, Roger is back again before the ticket booth has opened.

I know this because after he stopped answering his phone and didn't come to the door when I rang and rang his bell—even though his car was out front, his bicycle leaning against the wall under the window, where, on the other side, I stood on a flower pot crushing his lilies, just to make sure he wasn't lying on the floor dead—I spent the night in my VW Rabbit on the curb, and in the morning trailed his bicycle through traffic into the empty parking lot.

Only the week before, we'd visited the zoo together for the first time. It was a short break from studying, a treat. After three years in the English PhD program, we'd wanted to at last meet the animals we could hear through the woods from Roger's back porch. I realize now it was one animal: a primate. Often, if the windows were open when I stayed over, I'd wake to a clipped *Hoo-hoo-hoo* and find Roger smiling in his sleep. I should have noticed then. How he always goofed around before bed, acting the part of ape. There was a connection.

The afternoon we first went to the zoo, the sky was overcast, and it threatened rain. By the time we made it to the gorilla exhibit, the wind had picked up, and there was lightning. A handful of onlookers scattered from the fence, their children crying Bye! to the indifferent beasts.

Maybe we should go, I said, tugging Roger's hand. But he hunched his shoulders and scuttled about with limp arms, then pounded his chest, trying to get the attention of the gorillas. There were six of them, all with the same vinyl face and heavy brow, all hairy and dumpy.

Look, Roger said as he straightened up, a silverback.

Do you feel that? I held out my palm.

They're just like us, he said.

No, I said. They're smarter than us. They're all sitting under that rock outcrop.

Then it happened. Before I knew it, one of the hulking monsters was up on two legs and charging at us, banging her chest and roaring. For a second, I envisioned her leaping across the ravine and pummeling me. Then she stopped. I say *she* because of her enormous breasts—round, clay-baked breasts, upright and beckoning like a porn star's. She walked back to the rock wall and sat down and stared over her shoulder at me.

What the hell was that? I said, suddenly aware of my small chest.

Roger grunted.

Maybe she's jealous, I joked. Maybe she likes you.

He perked up. Come here, he said and kissed me for the first time that day. He turned me around and grabbed my waist and humped the back of my jeans.

Huh, he said. She's not responding.

I pulled away and ran down the path to stand under a small bridge. The rain was pouring down now. I yelled for Roger to get over here, but he didn't budge. He was blowing the gorilla kisses and doing some other stuff with his hips and arms. If it wasn't for the rain, I might have laughed. Instead, I screamed: What the fuck is wrong with you! You slob! You creep!

That did it. He came over to me, silent. The entire walk out of the zoo he said nothing. He got on his bike and left me in the wet parking lot. Then he stopped answering my phone calls.

For a while after I discovered Roger's fixation, I'd walk to the zoo and watch him with his chin on the fence, staring across the ravine at Malika. I'd bring him sandwiches and cry and stamp my feet. Why won't you leave this place? I asked. What am I missing? But he had no words left for me. On a bulletin board of pictures, I recognized his ape. The caption for the photo read: *Our newest arrival, Malika, is shy with the other gorillas and can usually be found exploring the habitat alone.* But, in fact, she sat staring blankly at the rock wall, seemingly unaware of her surroundings. I couldn't see anything special about her. And I had a feeling Roger faulted me for this. When I slid between him and the fence and pulled him close, I felt his neck straining to look over my shoulder at Malika. As if he were afraid that she might disappear.

I tried to be reasonable: Do you need space from me?

Forget what I said before, I bargained. I can wait. There's no rush.

Thirty's not so old these days, I told him.

He must have known I was lying. He spit the wad of sandwich he'd been working between his teeth over the fence; it smacked the edge of the ravine and dropped twenty feet into a muddy puddle. That was two months ago.

Now I spend my days staring into open books and not reading. I look over the three years I've been with Roger and search for clues as to what went wrong and how to win him back. On bad days, I wish I'd never come here, had stayed in Southeast Asia eating pineapples and selling braided necklaces on the street to tourists in Luang Prabang or Chiang Mai, where locals would point at my hair and say *sun.* I wish I never gave in to the fear of aimlessness that drove me back to school after traveling for two years, the fear that led me to Roger.

On good days, I think of him at orientation, how I'd flown to the Midwest directly from Bangkok, and next morning sat swamp-headed and gassy in a classroom overflowing with eager pronouncements of *ideology* and *hegemony* and *problematic.* How I, dazed and remorseful—What was I doing here with these people?—farted, for spite. Roger, sitting at the desk closest to me, looked over, startled, and then smiled.

I don't think I'd be here now but for that smile. In truth, Roger's teeth are the worst thing about his appearance: mottled and craggy, they turn handsome into homely. And yet Roger is, if nothing else, generous with his smiles. Or at least he was that first year I knew him.

I don't claim to be the same person I was back then, either. Not that it's clear to me who that person was or who I am now or when those two were no longer the same. Whoever she was, and whoever I am, is surely connected, in some way, with the pages and pages of books and books and books that now line my shelves. Before the PhD and Roger, I could fit my life into a rucksack I carried on my back. Now I'd need a U-Haul to get anywhere. It weighs on you after a while, all the stuff and worry. I don't say this to complain, only to point out that I could have, just as easily as Roger did, abandoned it all for a gorilla. But I didn't.

Whenever I can't sleep, I picture Roger alone in his house, sitting on his back porch or lying in bed, listening for Malika, his face blank with wonder, and I want to kill him. I ask myself: Is it enough, what he has with her? Will he ever want more?

I used to think it was enough that I loved somebody and that he loved me.

Or maybe I wasn't the one who believed this. Maybe some heroine from some imaginary somewhere did. Then again, maybe it was Roger.

In two weeks, he and I will be expected back for the fall semester. Already the people who have been asking me all summer where Roger is have started talking about their syllabi and schedules. These people are all married, some with kids. Before the theme of my nights became Where's Roger? it was Why aren't you and Roger living together? And just as I'm now, in his absence, made to answer for his whereabouts, back then Roger would walk away, pretending not to hear the question directed at the both of us and hunch his shoulders and smack his chest—pucka! pucka! pucka!—as if, in doing so, he might erase the question from my mind.

Not long before our trip to the zoo, he told me: I wish we'd taken things more slowly.

You? I snorted. You jump into everything.

He laughed: Good point.

Then I wondered: What did he mean? How much slower could it possibly get? Since our first month dating, during which he told me he loved me, wanted me to move in with him, and then, by the next month, took it all back, we'd been moving at a glacial pace, while everyone around us was getting engaged or having kids. It took him half a day to even respond to one of my text messages. Never mind living together. Never mind marriage. Never mind kids.

A friend from back home once told me over the phone: I don't think he's right for you.

What makes you say that? I asked defensively.

The way you talk about him, she said. You sound resentful.

Now, finding Roger exactly where I left him at the zoo two months ago, I wonder if she isn't right. Roger's light-brown hair has grown gnarled, his face overgrown with beard, the pits of his shirt greasy and wet. But in his silent limbs I sense the old unhappy restlessness.

What kept you away so long? he says without turning to greet me.

I decide against commenting on his need for a bath and join him at the fence. Are you planning to teach this fall? I ask and follow his gaze to Malika, crouched and digging a finger through the grass. *Slut*, I think. *Home-wrecker*.

I'm not planning anything, he says and licks his teeth.

Well, what should I tell people?

Screw people, he says. Haven't they done enough?

Right, I say, uh huh. So, I guess I'll leave you to it. Then I look over at *it*—Malika—and discover a baby suckling her giant breast. All at once the abhorrent image flashes in my mind—his white ass pumping the big-bellied creature—and I stumble back. Could it be?

You make me sick, I mutter.

I make *you* sick? He pounces on me. Look at me! Look!

And I do—at the ragged, worn face, the manic green eyes. I shudder. Let me go, I say.

If that's what you want, fine. He turns back to Malika.

It's what you want, I say.

If you want me to want that, he says, okay.

I want what you want.

Well, he says, I don't want what you want.

I say nothing. Together we watch the baby gorilla feed on her mother's breast. Roger takes my hand and puts it on his chest, like old times. God, he says, is there life in that big bust.

They say, I announce, that the flat-chested aren't to be trusted. They're cold, unfeeling.

Who says that?

All the great books.

Blameless

I have written this story too many times. The cast is the same, the drama, too. Brother. Brother. Sister-in-law. Sister. Sister. Boyfriend. This time, at least: no Mom, no Dad. No dogs.

Brother 1 (the eldest)—Moe—has two children now. Too young to be counted as characters. Symbols. Catalysts. They make this story sadder.

We're in Chicago here. At an outdoor concert venue: Ravinia. Our belongings include a sheet spread out on the grass, two coolers, three lawn chairs, a Pack 'n Play. We've planned for a long, hot Saturday in this sea of truncated people. Chicago, the band, will not perform until dark.

In the coolers: two thirty-packs of PBR; two five-liter bladders of chardonnay, their boxes shed…I'm forgetting what else—a handle of vodka? It doesn't matter.

This story happened years ago now. It isn't even my story. I shouldn't be telling it.

How it all started. Brother 2—Alan—abandoned us during the first hour. The quantity of alcohol we'd brought, Moe said, was figured, he said, dependent upon Alan's drinking.

Now Moe would have to pick up his pace. Make up the difference.

As it was, *with* Alan's help, we'd struggled carrying our stuff on and off the Metra, down and up the stairs. The coolers weighed like fire hydrants. And there were the chairs, our bags. The kids. All *their* shit. And now there'd be no Alan to help carry.

Plus, the sister-in-law was hammered, had been since before we'd left the house. And was useless, carried nothing when sloshed. Not even her damn purse.

Usually, in this not-uncommon scenario, the sister-in-law—Crystal—refuses also to carry her cell phone. And then, eventually, always, she wanders off and gets herself lost.

As soon as he notices her gone, Moe, the husband, sends out a search party. It is not a welcome duty. When we find Crystal, at last, two hours later, this is what she has to say, usually:

"Where the fuck were you? I've been walking around this fucking place looking for you fucks for hours! What the fucking fuck!"

There is no use, with Crystal, in pointing out that it was she who, for some reason and without warning, walked away from our spot. That our spot is still our spot, it hasn't moved. In fact, it's the same spot on the map we drew on a napkin for her when we sat down. The napkin, right there, in her pants pocket—*See?*—where we told her we'd put it, when it dropped from her hand onto the grass. No use in telling her we were worried, searched in shifts, our time ruined. We called her cell, but it rang beside us in the Pack 'n Play next to the baby, where she must have hidden it after Moe asked her to at least carry the phone if she wasn't going to wear her purse. No use in saying anything, no use at all, because she's pissed off, *mad*, and it's our fault.

Something you should know about Crystal: She isn't one to apologize. Not now. Not ever. She's a good Christian, raised by devout Christians. Thank you, God, Jesus. Amen.

Something else you should know: Alan has a low tolerance for Crystal. He lived with her and Moe in Chicago for three years before getting a decent job and finding his own apartment.

I don't envy Alan those years.

I don't envy Moe those years, either.

I don't envy Crystal.

Alan stands up, says, "Uh-uh. No. I'm leaving."

What has just happened is so tiny I have to zoom in, slow things down, rewind.

What has happened is Crystal groans. Crystal mumbles, "What the…"

You might have missed it if you were there. I almost did. It certainly wouldn't have been etched into my memory, even a minute later, if Alan hadn't declared his departure over it.

Alan is in a lawn chair before then. Below him, on the other end of the sheet, Crystal has just sat down. I think what happens, though it's hard to tell, is that she realizes that the warm sensation spreading across her shorts is beer. Maybe chardonnay. A spill no one has bothered to do anything about, let alone mention. In her place, I might have said something similar: "What the…" In fact, I would have been a real asshole about it, if you want to know the truth.

But Alan puts down his can of PBR. Alan says, "Uh-uh. No." Alan leaves.

And where is Moe? Off getting ice cream with his son, a three-year-old. His baby girl is napping in the sheet-cocooned Pack 'n Play between Crystal and the coolers.

"You're not really leaving, are you?" Sister 1 asks Alan.

"Please don't," Sister 2 says—*I* say. Sister 1 is my twin, Violet. We've followed Alan to the park's main exit. I tug on his shirt sleeve. "Don't go." My eyes sting with tears.

"I can't take her shit," he says. "It's starting already."

"Will we see you again?" Violet asks.

Alan lives half an hour from our brother. Once a year, Violet flies from JFK, I drive from Cincinnati, and we stay the weekend at Moe's house.

"If she's not being a bitch," Alan says, "maybe," and walks out the gate to the Metra.

Goodbye, dear brother.

Now Moe would have to carry the cooler Alan was supposed to carry. Full of the beer he was supposed to drink. Violet would carry the other cooler of alcohol, plus the diaper bag and a lawn chair. I'd carry the Pack 'n Play, Crystal's purse, a backpack, the other two chairs. Moe would have a cooler, yes, plus on his shoulders his son and, strapped to his chest, his baby girl.

Crystal would carry herself to the Metra. We could hope.

I don't want to tell this story. I'm sick of telling such stories. Sick, sick, sick.

And so, we have our inciting incident. And now we must lighten our load. Moe will be the hero. Throwing away full cans of beer, a bladder of wine—no, the thought does not occur to anyone.

Luckily, sort of, the boyfriend shows up during Chicago's last song. Moe couldn't have known the boyfriend would arrive, another person to help carry. No one knew.

The boyfriend—George is his name—was supposed to stay at Moe's this weekend, but his sister, who lives in Oak Park, cancelled her trip out of town at the last minute, and so he changed *his* plans last minute (on the drive to Chicago). Ditched his girlfriend. Me. His concert ticket purchased weeks earlier by Moe, who knew we graduate students couldn't afford it.

But the boyfriend comes through—arrives at the concert, feeling guilty about the wasted money, but not so guilty he'd avoid being eight hours late. That boyfriend shows up.

"Where's Alan?" he says. And Crystal sobs.

"It's not my fault," she says, looking at Moe. "I didn't do anything!"

(On our drive from Cincinnati, I tried to prepare George: "There's a reason all my stories are about my family." Though he and I had been together several years by then, he hadn't spent much time with them yet.)

Now it's time to go. The last Metra will be departing in ten minutes. George—who has just arrived on that train—slugs a beer, helps pack up our things.

It's a long train ride. George has time to slam another beer. George has time to slam a third, a fourth. George has time to imitate a gibbon. The toddler, my nephew, giggles. A woman seated three rows in front of us calls out, "Is there a monkey?" and stands and peers back at us.

When we get off at our stop, Moe says, "Where's our van?"

"Are you fucking kidding me?" Crystal, who was dozing on the trains, says.

Moe passes the toddler to Violet, and takes off down the street, the baby strapped to his chest. "I don't see it!" he hollers back at us.

"You're going in the wrong direction!" Crystal says and walks the other way.

"What!" Moe yells, a couple hundred feet from us. "What did you say?"

"That's not where we fucking parked!" Crystal, now a shrill voice in the dark, advises.

"I don't remember any of this!"

"That's because we didn't fucking park over there!"

"Jesus," George mutters, "someone's going to call the cops."

He, Violet, and I wait with the nephew near the stairs leading up to the train platform, all our belongings scattered on the sidewalk. We're in a residential area. It's nearly midnight.

"Didn't I warn you?" I say.

After Moe has at last found the van, loaded the heavy items in back, and is peeing in the bushes, and Crystal who knows where (passed out in the front seat?), I ask Violet, "Want to ride with us?" and she says, "They might need help with the kids," and ducks inside, slides the door shut.

I think you know where this is going.

Back in his own car, George revs the engine. George squeals the tires. George blasts through a stop light. "Ha-ha," George says.

"Don't be an idiot!" I say.

When does it cross my mind that none of us needed to drive? That we should have called for taxis? That, even though Moe has driven drunk before, this time he has his kids in the van?

When I answer my phone—namely, when Violet says, "Moe is being handcuffed. They're taking him in"—that's when.

"No," Violet breathes into the phone. "Don't pick us up. The cops are still here."

"What about Alan?" I suggest. "Maybe he's sober."

"He's not answering his phone."

The van is impounded. Violet and Crystal and the toddler and the baby take a cab back to the house, where George and I wait with the dog—a pit-bull mix.

(I was wrong. There is always at least one dog.)

"I told him to refuse to take a breathalyzer," Crystal says when they return. Thirsty is barking, his tail wildly slapping the coffee table. His nose dives into her crotch. "Stop!" she says.

Crystal is frazzled, she is crying, she is standing at the kitchen island in front of a laptop, looking up numbers for lawyers. She is blitzed.

Violet is upstairs, putting the children to bed.

"Thank god the kids didn't see anything," Crystal says. "They were asleep in the van."

"He watched the whole thing," Violet tells me, of our nephew, when she appears in the kitchen, "saw Moe get handcuffed, saw the cop car pull away with him in the back seat, crying."

Crystal is in the bathroom.

"What does he think happened?" I ask. "Is he upset?"

Violet shrugs. "He wanted to know if Daddy was sleeping here tonight."

When do children start forming memories? I wonder.

"Can we bail him out?" George asks. "Where did they take him?"

She produces a scrap of paper. "They gave us the name of this precinct."

"I need to find a lawyer," Crystal, back from the bathroom, blubbers. We watch her grope the mouse and stare blankly at the screen. "Fuck!" she says.

"Let's find the address," George continues, ignoring her, "and pick him up."

"Who's going to drive," I say, "you? You're going to drive drunk to the police station to inquire about a drunk driver?"

And where is Alan? Why isn't he returning our calls? We leave him frantic messages.

"I don't have my fucking phone!" Crystal says. "It's in the van!" She shoves the mouse. "How am I supposed to call a lawyer?" Forehead sinks into palm. "They took the fucking keys, wouldn't let me inside to get my purse, my wallet."

"Here," Violet says, producing her own phone. "Want me to dial for you?"

Crystal stays put on the couch, while the rest of us drive to the police station to bail out her husband. George has insisted that he's sober enough for the task.

In the car, I ask him to please obey traffic laws. I ask him to, please, when we get to the station, to please not park directly outside. I buckle my seatbelt and try not to think of the many ways in which his life could be ruined by a DUI.

"What happened?" he asks Violet as we pull away from the curb.

"I should have driven—it crossed my mind—I'd stopped drinking earlier—but I didn't want to risk it… I didn't realize how drunk he was at first."

"It's not your fault," George says.

"To be honest," I say, turning to look at her in the back seat, "I'm so used to—I mean, they can't even drive to the grocery store without bringing a beer or cup of wine. And Alan's always saying how Chicago cops don't arrest people for drunk driving…."

"Well," Violet says, "the cop seemed a lot angrier when he saw the kids in back."

Outside, orange streetlamps light the sidewalk. A public bus stops beside the curb.

"Why'd they pull you over?" George asks.

"He was speeding through intersections, squealing the tires. Scaring Crystal and me."

"Idiot," George says.

"*You're* an idiot," I say. "Remember?"

"We yelled at him," she continues, "told him to stop. That only made him go faster. Then I saw flashing lights in the back window."

"I can't believe he'd act like that," I say, "with his children…"

"I saw his eyes in the rearview mirror," she says. "They were spiteful, dead."

"Blackout drunk," I say.

The cop working the front desk at the station tells us that Moe was not booked there. He looks at the computer screen, his face a wall. "Where is he?" we ask. "Can we bail him out?"

"No," the wall says.

Back at the house, we climb the steps to the shared front porch and notice through the window Moe and Crystal's first-floor tenants watching TV on the couch. They look cozy, safe.

We unlock the door and head up the stairs to the second floor to find Crystal where we left her, staring vacantly in the darkened living room. George notices the upstairs porch door slightly ajar, closes it.

"They're making him spend the night in jail," he tells Crystal.

"You should get some rest," I add. "The kids will be up soon."

She shakes her head. "I won't be able to sleep."

"We can't do anything," George says, "until morning."

"This is so bad," Crystal moans. "The cop mentioned criminal charges. Moe could lose his engineering license."

"Is that the baby?" George asks.

Crystal cranes her neck to hear the wailing. Gets up and trudges down the hall into the kitchen, and then upstairs to their renovated attic bedroom.

Why haven't we heard from Alan?

Is he still angry with Crystal? Angry enough to not care that his brother is in jail?

Is he at his favorite local bar?

Is he passed out at home?

Is he lying unconscious on the sidewalk somewhere again? A group of men having spotted him, drunk and alone in the empty street—a target.

Will we get a call from a hospital in the morning—our third one in under a year?

The last police report included a quote from a witness who heard Alan say (he himself doesn't remember), right before a glass mug came down on his head, "Just don't kill me!"

What, I sometimes wonder, is rock bottom?

"She seems drunker now," George says, "than she was before we left for the station."

He and I are changing out of our clothes in the spare bedroom near the kitchen.

"I did notice," I say, "a wine glass in the sink."

"What a mess." He slides under the sheet in his underwear. "Did she go to bed?"

"I think she's watching TV in the living room." I sit on the mattress. "What if she passes out? Maybe I should stay awake. I don't think I'd hear the baby crying from down here."

His fingers trace my arm like a comb. "You should get some sleep."

"I'm afraid of what might happen to my niece," I say, "the way they've been drinking— Crystal falling down the stairs this past Christmas, knocking her front teeth loose... She'd just put the baby to bed," I choke. "I'm afraid to get attached to my niece, in case..."

"Maybe you should tell your brother that," he says. "Tell Crystal."

"What if she'd been carrying the baby?"

"Tell them."

I sleep but have bad dreams. The walkie-talkie din of emergency service responders fills the room. The window is open. A breeze wafts in, stirring the blinds, and with it, a man's voice, carried down the side passageway, citing an address—this address. My eyes pop open. It's sunny, morning.

In the living room, I hear a thumping on the door downstairs. I rush to open it. Several firefighters stand on the front porch.

"We were about to ram this open!" one of them says.

"Mind if we get up there?"

There's some pointing of fingers, and my heart dives into my throat: Crystal, my nephew, my niece. The firefighters push past me and jog up the stairs to the second floor.

Dazed, I follow. They gather on the upstairs porch, the door open. My mind lurches: What are they doing there?

I wait, arms crossed against the chilled air. The dog must be up in the attic with Crystal.

Then the firefighters are inside, swarming me like giant black and yellow-striped wasps. I feel exposed in shorts and tank top, my feet bare.

"Third flowerpot in Chicago this summer," the female says. "They seem to spontaneously combust."

"Oh?" I say, disoriented.

"You're lucky someone called it in," one of the men says. "The railing just caught fire. It must have been smoking all night in that soil, finally got hot enough and melted the plastic…."

For a moment, I picture an ember from a burning building, picked up by the wind and floating down the block, settling onto the soil in a flowerpot on our porch.

"Thanks," I say meekly.

Their eyes move off me and pass over the room, toys and clothes, cans, bottles scattered across the floor and on the couches and table. I don't live here, I want to tell them. This isn't me.

But they're already filing down the stairs, the tableau of a sleep-drunk mother dully standing amidst the evidence of her chaotic life still before them.

When the fire trucks are gone, I step out onto the porch. A thin trail of white smoke issues from the railing. Several plastic flowerpots still hang along its side, their plants shriveled and soil dry. *Spontaneous combustion*, I think. *Huh*, I think.

Then spot on the pavement below a smashed container, the dark soil like a pool of blood.

I go back to bed.

George and I wake late morning to the thumping of a kick-ball against the bedroom door and Crystal's "Stop! They're sleeping!"

"Is Moe back yet?" George asks when I return from the bathroom.

"No," I say.

Here is what we know: Alan was asleep when we called last night, had his phone off. He is coming over soon, Violet informs me. She has been helping with the kids for a couple of hours now. We haven't heard anything from Moe.

"What if he called my cell?" it suddenly occurs to Crystal.

We're in the kitchen, fortifying ourselves with coffee.

"Maybe we can contact the precinct," Violet suggests, "tell them to pass on a message—to call one of us instead."

"*Which* precinct?" Crystal says. "We don't know where the fuck he is!"

"I almost set the house on fire last night," Crystal mutters as I pass her in the hallway on my way to take a shower.

"What?"

"I was about to go downstairs and yell at our tenants—the porch railing is charred—but then I saw my broken flowerpot on the ground."

"There were firefighters here," I say, remembering the morning's events as if they were part of a dream. "The flowerpot caught on fire. They knocked it down. It wasn't your fault," I add, because she looks uneasy. "They said something about spontaneous combustion."

She gives me a strange look, and then walks toward the kitchen, grabs a broom, dustpan.

"Crystal almost burned us alive in our sleep," Violet informs Alan when he arrives. "Glad you finally made it."

She picks the baby girl off the living-room floor, pulls a safety pin out of her mouth.

"Uncle Al!" the boy squeals, raising his arms to be lifted.

"Shut up," Alan says to the barking dog. Then he collects his nephew in his arms and takes him, laughing, on a flight around the room, our little airplane boy.

"Usually I flush my cigarettes," Crystal is telling George and me in the kitchen. "But I saw you parking down below, and I panicked, didn't want you to see me smoking."

He and I are pouring ourselves bowls of cereal. Neither of us says anything.

"Since when," I tell George, "does she care if anyone knows she's been smoking?" I'm shoving clothes into a small suitcase in the bedroom. He and I plan to drive home this afternoon. I have to teach the next morning. "She and Moe light up whenever they drink, always have."

"Maybe," George says, "she had something else to hide."

"And I'm the one who had to stand there, like an idiot—those firefighters judging me!"

"This place is a train wreck," George admits. "Do they ever clean up after their kids?"

"That reminds me," I say, "don't use the towels when you shower. Apparently, they wipe up my nephew's piss with them when he misses the toilet and hang them back up on the rack."

George looks sick.

"I can't believe I'm the only one who heard the firemen," I say.

George heads back to his sister's. "I'll pick you up later today," he says and kisses me.

What, I worry, will he tell her?

Once, early in our relationship, I made the mistake of vaguely mentioning a dysfunctional childhood to his parents. Now, whenever I refer to my family in their presence, their moods shift, grow tense, expectant, and they murmur oblique remarks of sympathy.

What George almost certainly won't tell his sister: he was drunk driving, too.

It's remarkable how open George is with his family about *my* mistakes. He told them all about the time I was handcuffed in a Skyline Chili for grabbing a handful of extra complimentary crackers from the bin after eating a chili dog. Drunk, I wasn't aware of the group of police officers in a booth nearby, was easy prey, their practiced condescension successfully provoking me. I took offense at their suggestion that I'd contaminated the bin and their demand that

I pay the cashier fifteen dollars for the half-dozen oyster crackers—which I did, before I dropped the remaining three hexagons onto the counter and smashed them with my fist.

George was handcuffed, too, outside the fast-food restaurant, for requesting the arresting officer's name. I knew when he was put into the back of the patrol car beside me, his face stern, that I would not be easily forgiven, and knew, even then, that I would pay his citation, an attempt to appease him, which would in turn make me resentful that he didn't share my outrage for being mistreated. Yet I was relieved to have him there beside me, especially when the officer, taking pleasure in scaring "a couple of PhDs," informed me that I was lucky he wasn't bringing me in, because, he said, they would've inserted their fingers inside me. Rape apparently standard procedure and just punishment not only for taking six additional complimentary crackers without permission but for challenging the officers.

When George was handcuffed, they found a bowling trophy in his coat pocket, which he'd stolen from a bar earlier that night. Did he tell his parents that part of the story? No.

Thirsty is barking again. Someone is on the downstairs porch. We're all sitting on the couches in the living room. Hear the front door slam shut. See his head, then his body. Moe.

"How did you get here?" Crystal says. "Why didn't you call?"

"I jogged," he says, wiping his forehead with a t-shirt sleeve, "must've been three miles. I had to get out of there! I was going crazy. Where are the kids?"

"Napping," she says.

He sits next to her on the couch. "It was so cramped in that cell. I couldn't sleep."

"We tried to bail you out," Crystal says. "I called a lawyer."

"You were driving like an asshole," Violet says.

"With the kids in the car," I add.

His eyes rest on the open trunk of toys, its contents spilled across the floor like splattered paint. "I don't remember."

"It could be worse," Alan says. "Crystal almost burned the house down last night."

A few months into our relationship, George told me that his parents had recently asked if he was an alcoholic, said it ran in their family, they were worried.

I enjoy a beer or cocktail in the evening, he told them, that's all.

Whenever his parents visited after that, I'd make a point at dinner to drink only as much as they, a glass of wine, the whole time feeling, with the warm flush it brought, a sense of ease in their company, and fighting the urge to have another. I didn't want them to wonder about *me*.

Before I met George, I drank maybe once every week or two, and only when out with friends. With him, I took up the habit of a nightly soft buzz.

"It's a shame," his mother would say, over a plate of stir fry, in reference to my family.

"They've always been very supportive and loving," I'd correct her. "We're quite close."

"My brother's a drunk," his father would say, ignoring me. "My dad was, too."

What they never considered: Maybe that's why I love George. He brings me home.

Moe doesn't want to spend his first hours outside of jail indoors. It's half past noon, the sky ocean bright. We take the blue line a few stops to a street fair. From there, Violet, after spending a couple of hours checking out the arts and crafts, will take the train to the airport.

At the fair, Alan leads us through the crowd, past the food vendors and paintings and jewelry stalls, to a cordoned-off section. He orders a cup of beer and drinks it at a standing table, while the rest of us wait. The golden beer looks tasty. I consider buying one myself.

"I'm going to find ice cream for him," Moe finally says, and walks off with his son. Crystal stares at the ground, the baby wrapped to her chest. Normally we would all be drinking.

Before I can get a beer, Alan puts down his empty cup. "Let's find Moe," he says.

A few years after all this, when I'm thirty-five, I'll live for nearly a year apart from George, in Colorado. I'll feel as if I've been dropped in a desert, far from life.

Without much thought, without even trying, I'll give up alcohol. All desire for it gone.

When we return from the fair, Moe announces that he needs someone to drive him to the police station to collect his wallet and phone. Alan volunteers.

Violet must be waiting at her gate by now, should be boarding her flight to New York soon.

"When is George picking you up?" Crystal asks when we're alone.

We're sitting at the kitchen table. "Soon, I hope. I have to get up early tomorrow." I tear off a strip of newspaper, wind it around my finger. "Are you guys going to be okay?"

"I don't know." She stares at my finger. "The lawyer thinks it's good that he didn't take the breathalyzer. He'll lose his driver's license for a year but won't face criminal charges."

In the window behind her, the sun is low in the sky.

"We can't keep doing this," Crystal says.

"Drinking?"

"When I was pregnant this last time," she says, "I asked Moe not to bring alcohol home, and he didn't—for about six weeks. Then it was always here…I drank more than I should have."

"How selfish—why couldn't he go out to drink?"

"And Alan would bring over a twelve pack…" Her head droops. "Moe tried to stay sober the first time I was pregnant. But it was too hard, having Alan here living with us."

"Maybe the DUI will change things," I say.

"Maybe," she says faintly.

Alan got drunk his first time at one of Moe's parties. He was eleven, maybe twelve.

Moe once told me that he didn't start drinking, didn't really start, until college.

Eight years older than Violet and me, five years older than Alan, Moe would sneak us into bars whenever he came home, began doing so with Alan when he was thirteen, fourteen.

I drank my first beer while playing cards at the kitchen table with my family. The rules of the game required that a player drink each time a superior demanded it. Asshole, it was called. I sipped at the can, afraid. I was the Asshole, the lowest player. Was I thirteen?—younger?

"Drink," Dad, the Secretary, told me. He himself rarely drank.

"Yes," Moe, the President, chimed in. "Drink, Angie!"

"Drink," Alan, the VP demanded.

Mom, already drunk on her two warm cans of beer, laughed. It was all so fun.

(Wrong again: Mom, Dad—they're everywhere in this story.)

Moe and Alan, having returned from the police station, clatter up the back stairs and open the door into the kitchen. "When are you leaving?" Alan asks. He opens the fridge, grabs a beer.

"Soon," I say, standing up. "We were supposed to be on the road hours ago."

"*I'm* not waiting for him." He shakes his head. "Sorry." Then gives me a one-armed hug, pops open his beer, and drives home to his apartment.

Moe met Crystal at a bar when she was seventeen, a college freshman, and he a senior. Together, they became adults—codependents.

I met George when I was twenty-eight and starting the same doctoral program. Two years in, I told him, not for the first time, that I feared he didn't have any intention of staying with me after we graduated, and that, if it were true, I preferred that he break up with me now, not wait until I was thirty-three or thirty-four and my chances of meeting someone else and having children nil.

It was true, he finally admitted, that he'd always imagined we'd break up when one of us left Cincinnati, but it wasn't fair of me, he added, his voice shattered with hurt, to blame him for a childless future. Couldn't I see how unfair it was, pressuring him like that? He loved me.

And then, without our having resolved anything, he went back to his house and told his parents, who'd been visiting all that week, a version of our argument that contributed to their decision to give me, not him, not both of us, pamphlets on codependence they'd brought from church, which George, on his way to the shower, handed me after they'd left, saying simply, "My parents thought you should read these."

Only minutes before, I'd taken my toothbrush out of hiding, put my deodorant back in the medicine cabinet—a ritual I performed every time his parents left town. Now, stunned, furious, I dropped the glossy leaflets on his bed. From the bathroom came the sound of George, in the shower, whistling.

Had I known then that in five years I'd be teaching out in Colorado, waiting for my boyfriend of nearly seven years, back in Cincinnati, a thousand miles away, to finish renovations on his house before putting it on the market, waiting for him to join me and wondering, as the months wore on, his progress infinitesimal, if he ever would, if his unpacked boxes in the new apartment were a final ploy, a Trojan horse, threatening to reveal at any moment an assault on my trust, my love, would I have found the courage then, standing in that bedroom, the pamphlets like spanking paddles, the rage, humiliation rising within me as I contemplated them, while, from the shower, he whistled and sang—would I have weighed my love differently, acted on my urge to leave that house, that blameless man, without a word, and never come back?

Violet, by the time I write this, will be married. She'll say, "I don't know if I'll be able to visit you in Colorado. I might be pregnant by then."

George and I will have been together nearly six years when she says this. By that point, all our friends are married, having children—couples who've known each other half, a fourth as long as we.

"When is George returning for you?" Moe will ask me that Sunday evening in Chicago, long after Alan has gone back to his apartment and Crystal up to bed, the TV quietly bringing the two of us—my brother and me—someplace else for a while.

"Good question," I'll say. "That's the question of the hour," I'll say.

But before then, it is dusk. Alan, having hugged me goodbye, shuts the kitchen door and clambers down the back stairs to his car, an open beer in his hand.

"He brought a bottle with us in the car just now, too," Moe, seated at the table with Crystal and me, says when the door shuts, "was drinking his beer in the driver's seat while I went into the station to get my wallet and phone. The irony," he adds, "seemed lost on him."

"When are you coming for me?" I text George, knowing it will be late when he does. Knowing I'll have to teach my class on little sleep. Knowing I can't change anything.

Why are people always searching for the turning point in a story? Why must we limit characters, focus on one conflict, one resolution?

Well, this is no story. This is real. This is life. There is no resolution.

It all just keeps going on and on and on, in roughly the same way.

However Broken

God, I hated that fishing spot. One time, I had this toy that was from a cereal box—a big deal back then, since I was technically the youngest of four kids (my sister born ten minutes earlier), and even if I managed somehow to plunge a sticky hand into the Lucky Charms before my siblings, one of my older brothers would always snatch the prize from my fingers and tear open the cellophane. Anyway, I've forgotten the toy. When I close my eyes all I see is this green plastic thing, bigger than my hand, the wing of a plane, or part of a slingshot, a broken boomerang maybe—the remnant of a prize my brothers had destroyed and abandoned, no doubt—I see it tumbling through the air, smacking the stream below. I must have been perched on the ledge there. It was a good ten or twenty feet down, I remember, far—you can tell by the trees in the background, poking their heads out of the ravine. Which is what made it so odd a choice for a fishing spot—the distance, that is, between you and the water, the fish, if there were any. That day, I watched the current far below carry my boomerang under a culvert, and then it was gone. In my stomach, an injured bird flapped its wing. I cried. (Did I cry?) I asked one of my brothers to help get it back. (Did I ask a brother? I might have. I think I did. Someone, at any rate, at some point, said something like: "Impossible. It's too far down. Why did you drop it?" Maybe that's when I cried.) My parents called the fishing spot Number One—as in, I guess, the number one place to fish. What were their criteria, I wonder. Because besides the precipitous drop, there was also route 209 practically on top of us. It was dusty. Hot. I can think of ten other fishing spots, all of them closer to home, on back roads, quiet, quaint. Did we catch a lot of fish at Number One? Was that it? I have no memory of anyone catching any fish. Would such a thing even be possible from such a height? What was down there we wanted so badly? Often, I'd kick pebbles from the cement into the water. Scared the fish away, my brothers claimed—which earned me a punch in the belly. Or maybe it was my sister who was punched in the belly. That happens, you know, to twins. We absorb each other's pasts. What I want to know: Why is it, in every picture of my sister and me as toddlers, we're jammed under our mother's armpits like sacks of potatoes? What you don't ever get is the impression that she had any girlfriends giving her advice on how to raise twins. Not that she would have taken it. That's the thing with her: pride. When really, where does it come from? Look at us. Disheveled, cheap—like we were hatched from one of those plastic eggs in the vending machine at the Jamesway down the road from this spot. You know the kind of machine: that clucking chicken spinning atop a mound of toy-filled eggs, one of which, with the aid of a quarter, drops into the space behind the door, waiting for a hand to reach in and pluck it out, pop it open. "Can I have a quarter for the bock-bock 'chine?" my sister and I would chant, tugging on our mother's sleeve while she wrote some future (optimistic) date on the check she was making out for the cashier. Look at her. No bra. That hasn't changed. Birkenstocks. This was before she developed MS. When she could still wear loose sandals, high heels. Could apparently carry the equivalent of a bag of charcoal on each hip—and without losing her balance, tumbling down. If only I'd held onto this image of her, clutched it tightly to my breast. Who is that man passing the fishing rod to my father? I get the sense that my brother thinks he's a bit of a moron, whoever he is. Can't fix whatever's wrong with the rod. "Ha-ha," my father is saying. "Let me try." And maybe: "This is what I do half the time I fish: detangle their lines." My brother was a very bright and very serious boy. If he scowled, he must have had a good reason. Even if his legs bent back at a strange angle to his waist and his momma cut his hair with a bowl on his head.

The eldest of us, our brother, is probably the one taking the photo. He'd have a bowl haircut, too, the same one she always gave with the same salad bowl— our mother's gift to us:

predictability. Well, we didn't want it. She could keep it. We wanted to plunge our hands into cardboard boxes, to hold our fishing rods out over the expanse. We wanted to drop quarters into vending machines. Even if what we got was mostly disappointing. We wanted possibilities. If we lost a thing we cherished, however useless, however broken, we wanted to climb down, try to get it back. We wanted hope. Not some plodding train of a disease that year by year removed our mother further from us.

Fugitive Daydreams

It's somewhere in Nebraska. Bright out, early morning. You've just awoken in the passenger seat of a moving truck, your long-term boyfriend at the wheel, a buzz of apprehension battering your gut. For the past few days, between packing, loading all your belongings into a 26-foot box, scouring every nook and cranny of your apartment for the satisfaction of a capricious property manager threatening to withhold your deposit, and driving through the night from Colorado to North Dakota, you've caught only a few spells of sleep. It's August 2016. In seven hours, you'll arrive at your new home, a folk Victorian you've never entered, in Grand Forks, a town you never (before this summer) knew existed, in a state you've never wished to visit. What life decisions have led you here? Feeling like a fugitive, fleeing the worst year of your life.

An outburst, tears. Your boyfriend says *Come here*, and you unbuckle your seatbelt, slide across vinyl, feel the warmth of his arm on your shoulder. *Think how fortunate you are*, he says. *Not everyone*, he adds, meaning many of your academic friends, meaning him, *can say the same*.

Beyond the squashed bugs on the mammoth windshield: endless asphalt, cornfields. You miss the New York of your childhood, its trees, hills, winding roads—and green: absent from Alamosa, Colorado, as if even the color knew better than to settle there. But it isn't geography that makes you wonder if you've developed a form of post-traumatic stress disorder.

In a few weeks, you'll be starting another university position in another small, isolated town. Grand Forks isn't new to *him*, your boyfriend who, even now—as you fret over his parents' insistence on meeting you first thing at your new house (his parents' house, technically, paid in full with cash)—is stroking your back. You'll be living an hour from his hometown, a place he has no desire to live near, and in a region of the country that doesn't in the least appeal to him. Still, he says: *I'm proud of you.* No career opportunities for him where you're heading, yet he reassures you: *We'll make it work.* Middle-of-No-Where Colorado had nothing to offer him, either, but he agreed, if reluctantly, to move there too, after you'd been offered a tenure-track position—a dream for a graduate student. And now here he is, less than a year later, having to reconfigure his life again. Here he is kissing your brow.

After a while, you return to your side of the cab. Goosebumps prickle your arms, but you decide against turning down the air conditioner on your boyfriend again—he did, after all, drive all night—and instead hook a coat over your shoulders like a blanket. The shared cup of coffee, purchased along with egg sandwiches at a gas station, is tepid, its cardboard lip stained, damp.

Up ahead, a Camaro comes into view. As your boyfriend switches lanes and overtakes the vehicle, you catch a glimpse of the driver: middle-aged, Latino, elbow resting on the window frame, black hair snapping in the wind. The disparity between *you*—up in a massive truck that's hauling your own car behind it—and *him*—down below, seemingly motionless as you slip uphill past him—strikes you. You recall, all at once, having felt this sensation before—and what occasioned it: riding an elephant in Laos.

Delirious, no doubt, from exhaustion, stress, weeping, you feel the moment expand, synapses firing, as a succession of apparently disparate events from your past overlaps with the memory of the elephant ride. A writer, you fish a pen from your purse, confident that if you can capture the chain of thoughts, a pattern will emerge, coalescing into the shape of an essay. *What are you writing?* the boyfriend asks. You point to the speedometer: *Is that how fast you've been going?* Just below the speed limit. *Yeah*, he says. *I've been flooring it. Why?*

But how do you explain what is so far only a constellation of impressions?

*

You were deep in rainforest. Good: the setting. Start there. Two elephants waddling up a path through verdant foliage. Your twin sister called *Get one of me!* and you turned in your wooden seat to snap a photograph of her in an identical howdah, a bare-footed mahout straddling her own elephant's neck. Mirror images of each other. You smiled, in return, as she held up her camera.

After a while, the trees cleared, and you came upon a small circle of huts: a hill-tribe village—your destination. The path you were on led to the handful of small thatched-roof buildings and became a muddy track, which you, on your elephants, followed, doing a lap inside the shared dirt yard. Kids, naked or wearing only dusty t-shirts, stared up at you from doorways or from their interrupted playing while their mothers squatted nearby over large bowls on the ground, pounding rice. Mostly the women ignored you, but occasionally, one would look up and scowl, an unwilling participant in your ethnic safari, the backdrop her children, home.

You sat in silent horror, the camera in your lap. The tour took maybe ten minutes but felt interminable. An urge to get off the elephant seized you. *I'm sorry*, you thought. *I didn't realize.*

*

This truck, says the boyfriend—ever the astute doctoral candidate of English—*is the elephant?*

As we headed back, you say, ignoring him, *some kids chased us, threw rocks*. But even as you say this, you doubt the memory. Did that happen?

*

You were twenty-three at the time, a recent college graduate teaching English Conversation at a technical college in South Korea. It was 2004, summer. In the fall, you'd return for your second semester at Jinju International University, but until then, you'd have three months, paid, in which you were free of obligations. Back in late spring, a chasm of loneliness—more days just like this, weeks, *months* potentially of nearly-uninterrupted muteness in that small, conservative city—had seemed to stretch before you, and so you'd fled to Southeast Asia. Your sister, finishing her own degree in New York, would, it was decided, meet up with you a month into your travels.

And there the two of you were, all these weeks and several countries later, trampling over a hill-tribe village in southern Laos. To get there, you'd had to take a crowded bus on which a woman crouched in the aisle, hovering over a large basket of live, glistening frogs. A bamboo cage of squawking fowl had been loaded on the roof when you boarded and was set on the mud beside your backpacks when you arrived. Pigs roamed freely between the small huts. A monkey chained to a tree hopped between its branches. Women washed laundry in the brown river below. At dusk, monks in robes as bright as ripe oranges crossed a footbridge in single file, a waterfall serving as their backdrop. These were the sort of things you noticed.

What brought you there? Nothing, really. Chance. A paragraph in your guidebook. The vague notion of escaping the "beaten path." You were among only a smattering of foreigners in the village. The few restaurants and guesthouses seemed built in anticipation of more tourists. It was, in short, dead—nothing, apart from lounging in hammocks, to do. No cave expeditions. No slow boat on the Mekong with spectacular views of lush escarpments. No watching the sun rise over the spires of an iconic temple. No tubing by a riverbank full of bars selling buckets of beer.

Over breakfast your second day, you learned from the owner of a guesthouse about a tour guide who could take you on an elephant trek to a nearby tribe. By then, you'd been traveling for nearly two months, your sister for several weeks. There had been other elephant rides, other hill-tribe villages. Before she'd joined you in Bangkok, in fact, you'd trekked on foot for three days in the jungle of northern Thailand, slept in a Karen village near the Myanmar border. But this would be the first time you'd taken an elephant to see a tribe. (It didn't occur to you to ask *which* tribe, or whether they, like the inhabitants of that Karen village, would get a share of your fee for gawking at them.) *I'll arrange it*, the owner said. Earlier, he'd watched as a few guests fingered the rusty bomblets arranged like table decorations. You didn't fully understand their significance. Your guidebook had warned against leaving the paths when exploring lesser-known temples in Cambodia. And now here too, you learned, you must be careful. Unexploded Ordnances, UXOs. From the Vietnam War, you later read. Dropped from U.S. planes.

*

Before meeting your boyfriend seven years ago, you kept your life light, owned little, aside from books, that you wouldn't willingly leave behind. Now, as the two of you haul 1,600 cubic feet of your belongings, the Budget truck able to support ten tons of weight, you feel trapped by all of it: the stuff, the house, the career. Gone, the days when you could, with little preparation or thought, book a flight to another part of the world and move your life there. A prevalent theme of this past year's daydreams: escape. At your lowest point, you briefly considered how welcome a cancer diagnosis might be—a break from the constant dread of what other abasements and new depths of despair might await you each day in Alamosa.

What does any of this have to do with Camaros and elephants? the boyfriend asks now.

Hold on, you say. *I'm working towards that.*

*

You've already explained what elicited the memory of the elephant ride—that abrupt image: the man in the car down below, barely moving. What you haven't mentioned (the boyfriend is aware of it already) is that you've noted over the past few years, as the Black Lives Matter movement has gained momentum, an increase in media coverage of police brutality. Unarmed, unresisting Black and Latinx men and women, teenagers even, kids, being murdered by cops. Not a new phenomenon, except for its being reported in the news. *Do you think*, you ask the boyfriend now, *that he*—the man driving the Camaro—*was going so slow because he's afraid of what could happen to him, if he were pulled over?*

What you don't bring up is the fact that the job from which you're practically absconding is at a Hispanic-Serving Institution. Or that many of its mostly white students—some of its instructors, too—support the Blue Lives Matter counter-movement. During your year in the San Luis Valley, you met an unsettling number of people whose ignorance startled you, including a neighbor who, after giving you unsolicited teaching advice (he'd recently graduated from the college where you taught), waylaid you in the side entrance of your apartment while he gave lessons on, first, how Black people's brains work differently (nothing against them, he clarified, he had friends), and second, how the same is true of men and women. *Take this door hinge here*, he said. *When I look at it, I see... But you? And like, women wear pink—and purple.* He pointed to your tie-dyed shirt. His eyes were glassy, reminding you of the meth problem in town that he himself had warned you about when you'd moved here, nine months earlier. His hulking figure blocked the door.

One of your students—who also tended to stand domineeringly in thresholds (his feet just inside your office, for instance, as you sat at your desk and he held forth, once again, on a topic meant to demonstrate his superior intellect, a thirty-minute lecture punctuated by his informing you, erroneously, that he was your age)—told your colleague: *You're the only intelligent woman I've ever met.* As if it were a compliment. Yet, brilliant as your colleague indeed was, she was nevertheless on multiple occasions compelled to walk a student to her office to display for him her diploma, after he expressed disbelief, during class, that she held a doctoral degree.

Nearly ten years of graduate school and two terminal degrees, and this was how students addressed you: *Mrs.* The male faculty, even those without doctoral degrees, on the other hand, were invariably called *Dr.* or *Professor.* Administrators there made the same assumptions, as a caption of a photo posted online of you and a male colleague without a PhD makes apparent.

But here you are again, changing the subject, conflating your own situation with something you can't possibly fathom. White People Problems. Saying it doesn't make you less guilty. Saying it doesn't erase the fact that, minutes ago, you were crying, in part, because you fear that you might be leaving one nightmare, only to replace it with another, different one.

The plan at the start of the summer, as far as you'd known, was for your boyfriend and you to buy a house in Grand Forks. But at some point, without your knowledge, the plan shifted. His parents, who'd been critical of your top picks, began referring to the houses you toured with them as a potential investment of theirs. Your first house. You were to live in it, yes, and if you wished, could feel as if it were yours, but all your payments would go to them. What that meant to you: it was *their* house. His parents—who already influenced most aspects of their son's life. And who this morning had dismissed your request to have an hour alone in your new home when you arrived, calling it impractical. You wanted to return the truck this evening, they pointed out, didn't you? This was what had prompted your tears when you awoke in the cab: a suffocating, crushing fear. No autonomy. All the exit doors blocked.

Is it this lingering sense of claustrophobia that brings your mind, once again, to Southeast Asia and the man you met there? La. *Who?* the boyfriend asks.

I've told you about him, haven't I?

*

Nearly two months before that elephant ride in Laos, well before your sister flew into Bangkok, you were shaking hands with one of the guides on the three-day trek in northern Thailand. La, he asked you to call him. Only a few months before, he'd moved to Chiang Mai to join the trekking company. Your other guide, an older Thai man, met La, bright and charismatic, while leading a trek to the village, and recruited him. His English wasn't good, La apologized to the group; he was still learning—and trying to pick up French and German. No, a few people interjected, on the contrary, they were impressed by his fluency. When it was your turn to introduce yourself to the other Westerners, you noted, self-importantly, that you lived in South Korea, taught English there. La smiled and said fondly, "*Ajahn*," which became his nickname for you: Teacher.

Your first night of the trek, the small group sat at a picnic table at the campsite, drinking Chang Beer while La explained how he'd hunted at night with a flashlight as a kid. Later, after everyone else had gone to bed, he led you to the edge of trees and turned on his light, revealing what seemed like hundreds of tiny stars, the beam sweeping over the twinkling eyes of insects and animals otherwise cloaked in dark. By the time you reached the Karen village late the next afternoon, you'd spent two days hiking beside him. Your interactions were playful, childlike—swatting each other with branches, laughing—innocent enough for you to doubt he was flirting.

You were all enamored with La, talked amongst yourselves about how wonderful he was. A twenty-eight-year-old, he was kind, curious, handsome. The group asked about his childhood in a Karen village, learned that he'd hiked miles through the jungle to a one-room school, like the remote hut you'd been shown that evening. Every inch of paper was used, he explained; no white space wasted. There was no electricity or plumbing. An enviable life, some of you thought, charmed by the setting—the banana trees spotting the hill, verdant rice terraces and mountains in the distance—and the quaint stilt homes. It felt magical there, a time-capsule place. And you'd been permitted access to it, after hiking through the jungle for two days. As you all ate dinner on the deck of the tourist lodge that last night, you exchanged emails, promising to share photos and videos of the trek, nostalgic before you'd left the village or said goodbye to La.

*

In another week, traveling by slow boat through northern Laos to Luang Prabang, you'd meet Europeans at a guesthouse who, inspired by the setting (the village where you disembarked for the night had no roads and only intermittent electricity), would exchange tales they'd collected from their travels. An Irish man would say that he'd heard that if you went far enough north, you could encounter Laotians who'd run from you, screaming of ghosts. He was personally told this, he added, by a couple he'd met who'd experienced it themselves.

What happens, a Dutch woman asked, *after these kids see our digital cameras, realize there's a larger world out there? Will they want to see where the cameras come from?*

Are we changing the places we visit, someone else chimed in, *spoiling it all?*

The travelers at the table fell silent. *It's inevitable*, someone spoke after a while, *isn't it? At least we got here before everyone else.* Then the conversation resumed—more bragging about drinking snake blood; eating monkey brains; staying the night at a guide's home (instead of the hotel the man had arranged) to see where *he* lived, a one-room shack, and ending up sleeping on his bed while the man and his wife lay on the hard floor. Authentic. Explorers of "undiscovered" lands. Reenacting an old story—of colonizer and colonized. Not that you recognized that then, or your part in it. The privilege you had to move freely was not something you contemplated.

*

Sitting that last night in the Karen village on the deck, listening by candlelight to school children singing for you, the stars bright overhead, you thought: I could live here. With La. Raise a family.

Back then, you often found yourself daydreaming of a deserted island, far removed from your life. This time, you'd just finished a challenging semester in South Korea. A recent college student yourself, you didn't know how to teach. An introvert, moreover, you loathed performing.

But in this jungle, you thought, you could disappear. You'd already fled the States and the reality of being unemployed. And you'd fled, for the summer, Jinju, where kids would call to you in the street, "Hello!" "I love you!" and giggle behind their hands. But here, at last, you felt—moved by the singing, the stars—*here* might be a true sanctuary. La would be your savior.

*

Even now you sometimes catch yourself yearning for some imaginary somewhere far away. (*All the time*, the boyfriend says. *You do that all the time*.) You're surprised by where you've wound up in life—a teacher, the thought of being which used to make you cringe, and at the mercy of a dismal job market, moving from random town to random town. You went to graduate school to become a better writer but found yourself being funneled through their system, everything else slipping away—the writing now in service of the teaching. Tenure the new dream.

*

The point of all of this is the fantasy. The point is what happens next in Thailand. After you go to bed, dreaming of La, and that enchanting place. And after you awake, leave that village, hike out of the jungle, and return by van to Chiang Mai and the guesthouse that had arranged the trek. The point, what this whole tangent is leading to, is the next evening. When La knocks on your door.

Earlier that week, while still in Bangkok and newly arrived in Southeast Asia, you'd bought from a travel agency a package deal: the night train to Chiang Mai; a three-day trek; four nights at this guesthouse while you waited on a visa for Laos; then a slow boat to Luang Prabang with lodging along the way. La lived at the guesthouse, worked there when he wasn't leading a hike. After the trek, you'd seen him in a back office, smiled, and waved. When you phoned the front desk about a broken shower, he arrived—and must have assumed, after fiddling with the handle and finding that the shower worked fine, that it was a ruse; you'd meant to bring him there. He led you out onto the balcony, asked if you liked the view, and before you knew it, was kissing you.

And just like that, the fantasy ended.

You were taller than him by a foot; thicker in arm, leg, waist—despite your thin frame. It hadn't bothered you until he had you backed up against the wall. How long did you let him kiss you before ushering him out? A few minutes, maybe. Endless minutes. Filled with regret.

The next evening, he showed up at your door again. This time, he brought a plastic bag of street food—sticky rice, barbeque. What did you talk about while he shared his food on the small balcony? A football match he'd watched that day. His love of sticky rice. You don't recall what else. After you ate, he took a shower in your room (Was *his* broken?) and reemerged in a towel.

He pushed you onto the bed, slipped his tongue in your mouth, left it there, unmoving, a stick in mud. Tried to unzip your pants and, when you resisted, begged, "Try, *Ajahn*. Just try. Try." His towel fell open. (*Can we skip this part?* the boyfriend objects.) You thought of the VD clinic you'd seen in town earlier. No, you told La. And sat up. Kicked him out of your room.

After he was gone, you panicked. He could drop by unannounced at any moment; would know if you were there; you couldn't hide. You considered finding another guesthouse, leaving without saying goodbye, but worried that if you weren't there when the van came to pick you up for Laos, you'd be left behind and lose your passport, never mind getting the visa. There was no way you knew of to contact anyone, change your arrangements. You were, it felt, trapped.

Why didn't you just tell La how you felt? Probably it never occurred to you. You wish you could blame it on immaturity, inexperience, instead of your old friend cowardice. What you do recall is a thought you had shortly after La first kissed you, which was that you, who'd long felt invisible, weren't accustomed to having to face the reality of your daydreams, and that, contrary to what you'd once believed, it was awful, this power you apparently now possessed to turn longing into fulfillment—and that you ought now to be careful.[1]

____

[1] As you write this, another man in a later era of your life, whom you met in a different country, weighs heavily on your mind—this time, an American whose unexpected knocks on your bedroom window at

The next morning, you woke up determined to avoid La. You'd spend this last day, you decided, holed up in town, would read a novel in a restaurant and then a bar, and return to the room late at night; in the morning, you'd be picked up, at last, by the tourist van heading to the Laos border.

La watched you walk through the courtyard and out the gate. You lasted an hour in Old Town before he appeared on a motorcycle. You'd just finished breakfast and were sitting in the sun on the sidewalk. You cursed yourself for not remaining indoors. *Hop on*, he said. You told him no thanks, that you wanted to spend the day in town. But he persisted, until finally you got on the back. He drove you straight to

---

night would make you regret starting up with him, a man you hadn't initially been attracted to, but who'd worn down your resistance—so much so that, although you early on pretended not to be home, letting his knocks go unanswered, you'd eventually live with him, this man who—while you couldn't always stand him (how he'd intimate that you weren't as intelligent as him, or how he, depressed, would nap through a beautiful afternoon) and often threatened to move out (you weren't, after all, in love with him; and hadn't come to Central America, fresh off a breakup, to shack up with someone else)—a man who nevertheless loved you—but you had cared about him, hadn't you, even if you didn't want to admit it now, years later, even when he emailed out of the blue, writing that he hoped it wasn't off-putting for him to say so, but he was proud of you, and would love to hear from you, but understood if you chose not to reply—making you recoil and put off responding to him for eleven days before writing a flippant email about buying a house with your partner and accepting a better job than the one he was congratulating you on, a missive meant to communicate disinterest and rub in his face that you weren't, as he'd thought, or at least as he'd made you feel he thought (you sensed it came from his insecurities, a man six years older and not much better off), inferior to him—sending this reply in the midst of packing in Colorado, late on the afternoon of July 20—the same day (you'd realize two months later, as you, procrastinating writing this essay and curious why he hadn't responded to you, if it had to do with the partner you'd mentioned, indulged in an internet search, clicking on a website that spoke of him in the past tense) that he'd "passed from this life." July 20, 2016: the date of your email. He was forty-one, the obit also said. It happened "suddenly."

the guesthouse, letting you off outside the entrance before going in himself, so that his boss and coworkers wouldn't see you together. You returned to your room, defeated and furious.

As a young female traveling alone, you'd soon learn, you attracted the attentions of many local men, particularly those who worked in the hospitality industry. Easy, they must have figured, out for an adventure. Still, you think La was different. You know how that must sound.

How you went from pulsing frustration to a dreamy ache, you don't remember. Probably it had to do with your leaving soon—and the relief of not being cornered in that room. That last night, La borrowed someone's car, drove you to the countryside instead, where, in the warm blanket of darkness, you studied the stars, talked. He wondered what your lives would be like in the future, each of you on opposite sides of the world. His words were tender, wistful. He didn't ask to stay in touch. Did he kiss you? If he did, you probably didn't mind.

The next morning, as he was helping a new crop of tourists in the courtyard prepare for a trek, you walked past him on your way to the van. Your eyes met. Then he turned back to the circle, to whatever one of them was just then asking, and you walked through the front gate.

Probably he's still in Chiang Mai now, taking *farangs* into the jungle of his youth, foreigners who will afterward hop into a vehicle, heading to their next destination, "conquering" the world, bit by exotic bit, and later fly home to places La will never get a chance to visit.

*

Where all this is leading, you still don't know. You suppose it leads to taking an elephant ride to another hill-tribe village—in Laos, this time, with your sister. It leads to the same place, only this time so bereft of romance that you can't miss the ugliness of your being there. And all this traveling, these escape attempts—they lead to a rental truck in Nebraska, over a decade later. To your fleeing yet again one life for another. A life you already have misgivings about and think of as temporary. It leads to ten tons, if you want, of possessions in a 26-foot long truck box, more stuff than could probably fit, if laid out, in that shared courtyard of the Laos village you'd invaded while atop an elephant. It leads to a grown woman crying over a house her boyfriend's parents bought for her, complaining even as she slides uphill past a man driving a Camaro.

Aberration, that: moving truck outracing sporty car. Indeed, there is nothing natural about it, no intrinsic reason why you should ascend with ease, while others—like some of the Latinx students you're leaving behind who grew up in the San Luis Valley, one of the poorest areas in the country, and who will likely remain there all their lives—fear the consequences of simply stepping on the gas, knowing that somewhere an officer is waiting for them to slip up.

And yet, the boyfriend interrupts your monologue, *you remain a marvelous complainer.*

By now the reader will perhaps suspect that "the boyfriend" is an invention, a device. In the cab, your boyfriend says none of these things after he consoles you, though you do speak to him of the Camaro, the elephants, an emerging idea for an essay. *The* boyfriend is an approximation of *your* boyfriend, speaks like him, fulfills his wishes. *The essay*, your boyfriend will tell you after reading an earlier draft of this, *needs more connective tissue. The narrator should make explicit how it all ties together.* A fiction writer by training, you resist his advice, know intuitively that the pieces belong together. If you place them beside each other, the reader will do the rest.

No, the boyfriend says, *no*. Always no.

The boyfriend is an alter-ego. He tells you to shut up already. Get back to the essay. You're ruining it, he warns, undermining yourself, an already distasteful narrator.

For the boyfriend's sake, you pose a question: How will you get the reader from here, on this highway, contemplating the relativity of freedom, and a decade-old, tawdry tryst featuring a man with the improbable name La, back to a year you've designated as the worst of your life?

*

That brilliant colleague of yours, the only faculty member in Alamosa you befriended, faced resistance from students who, when subjects such as white privilege arose in class discussions, would fold their arms, grumbling: *What privilege?* One such student even complained on the course evaluation that the professor, an obviously white woman, was racist against white people. Why did Black Lives Matter, her students would demand. Why not *all* lives? Saying this in front of their Black classmates. Once, a Black student of hers expressed surprise that a white woman was acknowledging that racism exists. He'd never heard a white person say that.

*

Two weeks after your boyfriend (not *the* boyfriend) and you—with his parents' help—unload the truck and move into your house in North Dakota, you'll attend a new faculty orientation in which a seasoned professor on a panel offering advice will say, *It's okay, in fact it's a good idea, to tell your students, "I don't know."* Hearing this, you'll feel an urge to snort. You believed that too, seven months earlier—that is, until you said those words to your students in Colorado.

*

Early that spring semester in Alamosa, a student asked you what the spider symbolized in a novel you were reading, *Palace of the Peacock*, written by Wilson Harris, a postcolonial theorist and writer whose fictional work subverts hegemonic reading and writing practices, undermining the Western literary tradition's prioritization of clarity and linearity. Harris's work forges new ground for a Caribbean approach, one that destabilizes time and language. It's characterized by many Western literary scholars as challenging and opaque. The spider the student referenced makes a brief appearance. Still, you'd wondered about it, too, had searched the college library's limited database to check if anything was written about it, and found nothing. But your student, frustrated with the difficult novel, wanted an answer. She didn't appreciate being told, "I don't know." In fact, this admission of yours became a major source of concern for this white student and her friend who wrote, when you asked for "anonymous" feedback (it was handwritten in a class of six) midway into the term, of their vexation with your saying *I don't know.*

Your consequent attempts at opening a discussion on student-centered learning, which included reading together in class an excerpt of Elaine Showalter's *Teaching Literature*, in which instructors are cautioned against offering students a "golden key" to interpretation, only made the situation worse. It didn't mitigate their ire, either, when you explained that you weren't reading canonical texts, and that, in some cases, there wasn't a body of scholarship on the works yet, and so it was up to the class to pose questions and develop interpretations. This, you reasoned, was the foundation of literary scholarship; it wasn't an exercise in plugging in pre-packaged answers. How, you wondered, could these students, English majors, not recognize that?

You hoped they'd reexamine their assumptions, but your attempts to reach them failed. They became what teachers sometimes refer to as "toxic students," brazenly grumbling or rolling their eyes about reading assignments, quizzes, in-class work; noisily walking out of the room to use the bathroom as you spoke. They couldn't, it seemed, tolerate a lapse in authority. Evidently, you weren't supposed to admit you didn't know.

*

And now, fast forward months later, and here you are, at an institution recommending to its new faculty a course of action that directly led to the worst teaching experience you've ever had. But you agree with their advice. As a graduate student, you often heard professors say those words, and appreciated it, the way it seemed to demystify the learning process, allowing you access to the lectern. Had your students never heard any of their instructors admit that they didn't know?

*

The week after the faculty orientation, you will discover that, for the first time since you began teaching, you have no students of color. Did that account for the faculty's openness? And did the mostly white faculty at the college in Colorado feel an unconscious need, with their more diverse student population, to maintain their authority? Wondering this, you'll be reminded of what you heard faculty members in Alamosa sometimes say: it felt like they were teaching high school. It was true that most of your students (even the

120

English majors, especially the two who disliked you) didn't read the assigned texts, even when they were on reserve at the library and cost a few bucks online. True that some of your students didn't bring paper or a writing utensil to their writing courses. True that in every class, five to ten students would walk out to use the bathroom for ten to thirty minutes, regardless of who was then speaking. But why were you told to expect this, and to work around it, and that your students would be unmotivated and disappointing?

Near the end of your first semester in Colorado, the chair of the English department met with you to discuss a composition course of yours he'd observed. After telling you, without elaboration or advice, that the class had been "okay, not great," an apparently grim assessment, he brought up a different course, introducing the subject by saying that when he'd asked a few of your students in it how the class was going, none, he stressed, had used the word "love" to describe their feelings about you; in fact, he added, one had even said your voice was monotone. You therefore needed, he urged, to do "triage," which, it turned out, meant you should bring doughnuts and cancel the last few classes. Not surprisingly, the man dispensing this advice was himself hated, you'd heard, by many of his students. A spiteful buffoon, he nevertheless had power—and would soon, along with a few other colleagues (one of whom, a flagrant misogynist and sexual harasser, had already given you reason to worry), be meeting for your one-year review. Student evaluations, you knew, would weigh heavily in decisions regarding renewing your probationary contract.

The following semester, after you'd told one of the toxic students, who'd been five to fifteen minutes late to six classes in a row, that she needed to arrive on time, she coldly informed you that other professors didn't count it as late if it was under fifteen minutes. After this encounter, she formally complained to your colleague friend about your telling the student that she needed to arrive to class on time. Then she cited, as a serious infraction, your saying you didn't know what a spider symbolized in a novel a couple of months earlier, and even asked this professor, who'd never heard of the novel, if *she* knew what the spider meant.

Not until you, worn down and worried about tenure, told this student and her friend that their grades were in the "B range" (this was somewhat true of one of them; the other's was closer to a C) did they apparently decide (they told your colleague friend) you weren't so bad, after all, turning their wrath instead on another professor, you'd later learn, whom they also feared would give them bad grades. Terrorizing him, surely, in the hope that he, too, would change his mind.

This, it seems, was the sum of their higher education. In fact, they boasted to their peers that they never did the assigned reading in any of their classes and would simply "bullshit" their way through, earning an A or B for their efforts. These two would graduate in a couple of weeks (one of them) and a year (the other), as English majors, having read, according to them, next to nothing. Both girls were white. At what point in their education had they come to think of themselves as entitled to A's and B's, without having to honestly earn them? In the end, you helped them in their mission, did them the greatest disservice of all.

*

That's what all this is about, isn't it? The damage we do without even trying.

*

Have you learned so little over the years? Are you the same person, bumbling upon that village, glued to the back of an elephant, afraid to apologize, tell La the truth?

You're asking me *this?* the boyfriend says.

*

You began this essay before the 2016 presidential election was decided, wrote most of the above and some of what follows before the shock of Trump. While journalists report that white voters chose him not because of but despite his bigoted remarks, their frustration with the economy and government eclipsing concerns about racism, white privilege comes again to mind.

*

The man you didn't love who is now dead once told you that he'd consider himself having led a successful life, not if he'd helped others, but rather, if he hadn't caused them harm. He preferred the don't-interfere-in-other-people's-lives approach. You wonder about the wisdom in that.

It took you eleven days to respond to his email, for instance, after seven years of silence, after you'd found that your memories of him, that relationship, disturbed you. You were dating him when Dr. Henry Louis Gates, Jr. was arrested after being accused of trespassing in his own home. It was before your PhD program. You hadn't taken a course in postcolonial theory, didn't understand how systemic racism works, didn't know the term *implicit bias*, hadn't even heard of Gates. But when the man you didn't love defended the officer who'd harassed and arrested a professor in his house, noting as an aside his sympathy for cops and their use of racial profiling (*Look at the incarceration rates,* he argued. *I understand why cops get scared, pull the trigger, especially in some of those neighborhoods*)—and when he said (after he learned that your ex was Korean) that interracial relationships were doomed, we were too different—you recognized what he wouldn't ever acknowledge, maybe even to himself. And it was hard to love someone like that. It was hard even to admit you'd been in a relationship with him.

You have over the years had dreams about this man trying to insinuate himself back into your life. The dreams have the quality of nightmares. When he sent that email in July, you broke into a cold sweat. It took you eleven days to respond. And now you'll never know if he read that email, or if he died assuming you'd chosen not to reply. You'll never know if you shouldn't have sent it, or if you should have sent it sooner, or if it didn't matter. You'll never know—and you'll never be quite the same. And it doesn't make a difference if he didn't intend to cause you harm.

*

You've long since left Nebraska, skirted up the side of South Dakota, and crossed the state line, Fargo behind you, when it happens, sometime in the early afternoon.

Your boyfriend and you, high up in the truck, see through the enormous windshield a black-speckled cloud dropping onto the road like a hut in the clutches of a tornado.

What's that? you say the instant before the truck plows into it.

A sound like a popping burst of rain. And then it's gone.

Hundreds of translucent, yellowish smears dot the windshield—honeybees, you'll know for sure later that afternoon, as you pluck carcasses from the wipers and wash the sticky residue.

You would prefer not to have massacred the bees, of course. But you'd had to transport all your many belongings to your new home, that seemed important, and it necessitated using a big truck.

Hours later, after you clamber onto the hood and scrape away the remains, you will return the moving truck in Grand Forks. Then you'll drive back with your boyfriend and his father to your new home, where your boyfriend's mother waits, exhausted from carrying your boxes into the house, technically her house, which she diligently cleans, a seventy-year-old who loves you, and wanted, like her husband, to greet you when you arrived, even though you'd wished they wouldn't.

*

A lesson in all of this, somewhere.

*

An idea—something you propose for yourself before you teach the next crop of students: less selfishness. Less avoidance of discomfort. Some courage, damn it.

And gratefulness, the boyfriend proposes.

Yes, you say. *Thank you.*

Less complaining.

All right, all right.

*

Here is the point: this essay is at last almost finished and already you want to drag this file, with its hideous self-portrait, into the trash bin. But you can't, because it's four-and-a-half years later, you're still in North Dakota, your boyfriend is now your husband, you have an infant, too—and you're coming up for tenure, need the publication. It's too late to start from scratch. Even if you did, the same selfishness would appear, this time as the backdrop to COVID-19 and the stark racial inequities it's highlighting, as people—white mostly, some gathering with Confederate flags and swastikas, nooses and rifles in large numbers and without protective masks—protest the loss of their freedoms,

125

while their black and brown countrymen are dying across the nation in terrifying numbers, on pavement and in cars, as ever, and now too, increasingly, in hospitals and homes, even as you write this last insensitive, serpentine sentence, hoping the virus doesn't shut down too many literary journals, so that one of them will agree, at long last, to publish this, and you can say to the boyfriend (now the husband): *Why didn't you stop me from sending this out?*

Probabilities of the Unde(r)served

As a work gets more autobiographical, more inti-mate, more confessional, more embarrassing, it breaks into fragments. Our lives aren't prepack-aged along narrative lines and, therefore, by its very nature, reality-based art—underprocessed, underproduced—splinters and explodes.

—David Shields, *Reality Hunger*

I remember: "Why are they *so skinny?*" I remember he used the word *disgust.* I remember how he seemed to relish tell-ing me that the sight of us twins—pot-bellied toddlers, then stick-figure teens, adults—had always turned his older brother's stomach. The mere mention of our names, he added, could do it—cast that look across his brother's face: disgust.

I remember his wife was in the bathroom at the baseball stadium as he revealed all this.

Only a few months earlier, he'd confessed to me: "I'm in love with you."

I'd scoffed. We hadn't so much as kissed since I was a teenager and had hardly stayed in touch. Apart from some basic facts about my life, he barely knew me. "What about your wife?"

"I can be in love," he said indignantly, "with two women at once."

"And she's okay with that?"

"Bella wouldn't understand," he admitted, "something like that."

What made him think that *I* would?

My brother's best friend. Ron. Practically raised me, eight years younger than him.

Now, three months later, he was letting me know that his wife *also* thought we were too skinny. "You," he added, "especially."

When Bella returned to the bleachers, I felt an urge to cover up, despite the blistering sun.

I remember: All this took place two summers before that older brother of his would dive at me in the dark, his arms straight like submersible robotic manipulators, groping, on the way down, at the terrain, fistfuls of boob, small as they were, skinny as I was, disgusting.

A family affair.

Even their greasy-headed, skeleton of a father had a go at me. "I heard you want to be a writer," he said. I'd just started an MFA program in New York City. "Better get used to holding a sign: 'Will work for food.'"

My family was at their house to celebrate his younger son's safe return from Iraq. Earlier that day, out on the deck, Ron had casually remarked, as he chewed on a hot dog, his wife in the house, "I told my dad you're a literary genius. He'll respect that. He's a huge Mark Twain fan."

Literary genius. Did it matter that he'd never read anything I'd written?

That night, his father grabbed my hand, yanked me off the couch. Tried to slow dance. Told me, no, he didn't want to dance with his wife, she was repulsive. Said he'd run off with a young thing like me, though. If she were deserving.

Which we all know I'm not.

But some will take it anyway. They're not too particular.

*

Just ask this other septuagenarian: Mick Goldwater. Professor of my first writing course. "My initial impression of you," he said as we sat alone in his office, a configuration I'd steadfastly avoided, until now, my last semester, when I had to meet with him to discuss my thesis, "was that you weren't very bright." But then, he said, he'd seen my feedback on another student's story, comments I'd written in the margins. "I was wrong," he said now. As if proffering a gift.

In his fiction class three years earlier, while, for the first time ever, a short story of mine was being workshopped, and I listened silently, as was the custom, Mick (he'd asked us to call him) said something I didn't catch. The other graduate students tittered, shifted in their seats.

I looked up. Their eyes fell away. "What?"

At the other end of the seminar table: Mick, plump fingers splayed over my manuscript. But the moment was over; the discussion had resumed.

"What did he say?" I whispered to a classmate near me at the seminar table. He made the gesture of one gagged by decorum: the professor was speaking.

So I returned to my note-taking. And soon forgot the incident.

Months later, another classmate brought it up: "I can't believe Goldwater *said* that." We were sitting on stools at the bar. "Said what?" "You didn't hear him?" "Tell me." He picked up his pint glass. "You don't want to know." Shaking his head.

We'd all heard the rumors. An employee at the Strand Bookstore, for instance, knew of a student who'd gotten crabs from Mick Goldwater in the 80s or 90s. No one was especially surprised. His commentary in workshop consisted of regaling us with his sexual fantasies, sometimes about his own mother, as she'd lain in bed, some years earlier, dying of cancer. Other times, he'd openly contemplate breasts in the classroom—those belonging to a student who'd sit at his elbow, for instance. "I can't blame him," she'd tell the rest of us as he openly ogled her, "they're huge!"

How she came to be one of his (usually male) devotees: she'd attended his class the first evening by mistake, had enrolled in a poetry workshop and confused the classrooms, but stayed put after realizing her error and found herself so taken by that class that she switched not only courses but genres. No longer a poet, she'd interrupt discussions of her work now to tell us, "An editor will fix that." Mick was unusually quiet at such times. Other, better, writers suffered his simultaneously tearing apart their stories while complimenting them on their flattering tank tops.

If his dear wife's name passed from his lips, it was generally in the context of baking (a Tupperware bin of fresh rugelach on the table beside him) or post-menopausal women: revolting.

It's hard to imagine a professor getting away with any of this now. But none of us questioned it. A fixture in the program, he had a reputation for mainly one thing: brutal honesty. That's the only warning I received when I registered for his class: if he didn't like your story, he'd tell you.

"Write what scares you," he famously advised his students, "the dangerous story—what you don't want to tell." He pushed for autobiography. "Where are *you* in this?" Sex scenes, we noted, were especially well-received, and who among us didn't want to hear, "You're talented"?

In truth, it's not hard. To imagine. Even now. I know of other professors—*worse*. Universities quietly dispatching large sums of money defending them in sexual-harassment lawsuits. "Etcetera, etcetera," as Goldwater was fond of finishing his own sentences.

In many ways, I'm still back there, at his seminar table. One of my classmates is saying, "This is the best line, right here." He's reading aloud the part where the girl rolls off the guy and falls asleep, rather than walk a few steps to the bathroom's plastic door and suffer his hearing her pee.

"After I read your story," another classmate (the one who later told me, *I can't believe Goldwater said that*, and who'd eventually confess his feelings for me) wrote in an email a few days after that workshop to apologize for his "awkward rambling" in class, a rambling I couldn't, in fact, recall, "I had a dream. The scene with you not peeing—after, you know? Let's just say it came up." The not peeing, in the story, leads to a UTI that leads to pyelonephritis that leads to a hospital stay in South Korea. Fiction. Not personal essay, not memoir. Not *me* not peeing.

"It's not plausible," an older woman from class had told me at the bar after our workshop. "Girl her age—" she said, "in her early twenties? Not knowing about UTIs? It'd never happen."

"Right," I said.

Months later: "You don't want to know," the guy who had *feelings* decided for me, regarding what Goldwater had said months earlier about me, in front of me, to all my classmates.

What he, the smitten guy, didn't know, and what I knew better than to tell him, was that Goldwater, editor of a literary journal, had offered to publish my story right after that workshop.

And years later, as I sat across from the man in question, waiting to receive his feedback on my thesis, he had something else to offer me: a confession.

"I have a crush on you," Goldwater said.

Was that before or after he told me I wasn't bright? Before or after he opened a drawer and handed me the first issues of the literary journal he edited, in which early stories by Donald Barthelme and Italo Calvino and Samuel Beckett appeared, and said: "Don't tell anyone I gave you these"?

"You remind me," he said languidly now, "of my Scottish nanny." Black eyes glinting. "Boy, did I fantasize about her." Hands behind his head, studying me. "How old are you?"

Twenty-seven. Twenty-four when we met, nearly a third his age.

When he'd offered to publish the UTI story, he assured me, unprompted, in an email, "I had my wife read it. I always do that," he added, "so I know I'm not biased."

But after I submitted my second story for workshop, he asked to publish that one instead.

"You do realize, of course," the skeptical older woman from workshop confided in me at the bar after Mick had some weeks earlier told our class that we wouldn't be discussing the story, he was going to publish it as is (though he'd emailed about swapping stories, his announcement caught me by surprise, made me uneasy), "it's not a very good story, right? We were all talking about it the other night," she added, rattling off names, including the guy who'd long since declared his feelings for me and was by now infatuated. "Everyone agreed—" she said, "it needs work."[1]

My first publication.

A crush on you.

What do you say, in the face of wildly inappropriate, preposterous confessions? What do you say, when you're in your twenties, just a kid? When you feel beholden to the confessor? ("Your classmates will be jealous," he'd warned you. "I haven't published a student in years.") What do you say?

You say nothing.

You don a carefully cultivated deafness.

You change the subject—back to your thesis. "What did you think of the last story?"

Then one day you find that you're still trapped in that office. You watch yourself, years later, fall into a familiar, anguishing dumbness, whenever the professor you most admire in your doctoral program talks with you outside of class. "Is something wrong?" he asks the first few times. Then stops asking. You want to be professional. But here you are. It started after he emailed to tell you that your contributions in class were swell. And after he nominated your work for a literary prize. You know of only one reason a professor would do such a thing. You've been a student elsewhere, and you've always been a good student; you've learned every lesson your teachers have wanted you to know. Not bright,

---

[1] Trinh T. Minh-ha describes such moments in *Woman, Native, Other: Writing Postcoloniality and Feminism:*

> To capture a publisher's attention, to convince, to negotiate: these constitute one step forward into the world of writers, one distress, one guilt. One guilt among the many yet to come, all of which bide their time to loom out of their hiding places, for the path is long and there is an ambush at every turn. (9)

the last one said. This one, the one you admire, decides: Not assertive—which is what he (you'll later learn) tells a search committee years later when they call your references. You won't get an interview for that job.

"The last story?" Goldwater reluctantly returned to my work. It was a story another professor, Finn Holt, had offered to help get published (after which, he sublimed like dry ice, ignoring my email with the revision he'd requested, and my follow-up email—only to be deposited briefly in the hallway the next year, a passing substance, calling: "Send me that marvelous story!" which I did, again, to no avail). "Cartoonish," Goldwater dismissed it now. "What does it have to do with you, a talking house?"

Everything. The house my house. The mother my mother. Her shame my shame.

I wrote it, I also didn't tell Goldwater, in response to Holt trashing my first story. He only praised, I came to notice, the unexpected, the uncanny. Realism bored him.

"The other stories," Goldwater added vaguely, "are good."

He'd read earlier drafts of many of them, including in another class I'd taken with him—a requirement, he'd let me know, of his chairing my thesis committee; two classes, he'd implied, was barely enough. But no one else, my peers agreed, would write as many comments as him on our theses. No one else would take the time. As well as being a harsh critic, he had a reputation for caring about our work. He knew, he said, what his feedback meant to us; he respected that.

Good? I waited for Goldwater to elaborate. He'd particularly liked, I remembered, the story about a man who preys for years and years on a much-younger girl and her twin, practically his sisters, still teenagers. But it was a long story.

I'd submitted it late. His workshop letter had focused on bewitching sensuality, etcetera, etcetera. He didn't write on the manuscript itself.

Still, I'd gotten an A in the course. No one else had gotten an A. Not even his devotees.

I knew my audience.

In her essay "On Pandering," Claire Vaye Watkins writes, "It was Toni Morrison who pointed out that Tolstoy was not writing for her, who said she was writing toward black women. It makes you wonder, Who are you writing for? Who are you writing toward? Myself," she continues,

> I have been writing to impress old white men. Countless decisions I've made about what to write and how to write it have been in acquiescence to the opinions of the white male literati. Not only acquiescence but a beseeching, approval seeking, people pleasing. But whom do I mean when I say white male literati? … I mean the people and voices real and imagined in the positions of power (or at least influence) in writing and publishing, but mostly I mean the man in my mind.

And, too, Wakins means, as a 'for instance,' a professor in her MFA program. A man who'd encouraged her, called her a great writer. "I am speaking," she adds,

> not of Lee Kitteridge Abbott the man but what he represents. Or rather I am talking about them both, about the representation and the man himself, for didn't I know he would like that story, about an old prospector who finds a nubile young girl left for dead in the desert? Glad you like it, Lee. It's *for you.*

Watkins is describing above something that happens in workshops, but she is also describing what it has meant, for some of us, for most of our lives, to be readers and writers of literature.

"You wouldn't like it," a boyfriend in my MFA program told me after he borrowed my new copy of Michael Chabon's *Cavalier and Clay* before I'd read it, and then claimed it his.

"Why not?" I asked, genuinely curious.

"It's too male-focused," he said.

I wondered what he meant. Was it misogynistic? Then I read it and did, in fact, like it.

What did he think I, an English major in college, like him, normally read?

Yet here he was again, telling me I'd hate Nicholson Baker, Don DeLillo. He did, however, suggest I read Mary Karr's memoir, *The Liar's Club*.

He meant it, I intuited, as an insult. To put me in my place. Even if he didn't recognize it as such. My childhood, he'd told me, sounded like Karr's. Simple as that.

And the rest?

Watkins: "I am trying to understand a phenomenon that happens in my head, and maybe in yours too, whereby the white supremacist patriarchy determines what I write." She asks herself why she imagines, as her audience, Philip Roth instead of Karen Russell, Jeffrey Eugenides instead of Antonya Nelson—why she unconsciously seeks, above all, the approval of male writers (and, by extension, male critics), some of whom wouldn't give her own work, for sheer reason of her sex, a cursory glance (*see also* Norman Mailer). Why does she *do* this?

Perhaps because she received the same education as me.

Perhaps because, as Francine Prose outlines the problem in her essay "Scent of a Woman's Ink: Are Women Writers Really Inferior?," male writers of literary fiction win the big awards, appear in the major magazines, get reviews in serious journals. They're the ones afforded the time and money to write. "To ask," Prose writes, "what effect critical neglect has on the careers of women writers is rather like inquiring into the health of the female population in cultures that place girl children at the bottom of the food chain."

Watkins writes for men, in other words, because she wants to survive. It's hard enough being a writer without that accursed adjective, woman. But, Prose asks,

> Is fiction by women really worse? Perhaps we simply haven't learned how to read what women write? Diane Johnson... observes that male readers... "have not learned to make a connection between the images, metaphors, and situations employed by women (house, garden, madness), and universal experience, although women, trained from childhood to read books by people of both sexes, know the metaphorical significance of the battlefield, the sailing ship, the voyage, and so on."

No coincidence, then, that Watkins titled her collection *Battleborn*, signifying to the male literati: This is good—important. It isn't fey. "It's all an architecture of pandering," she explains. "It's *for them. She can write like a man*, they said, by which they meant, *She can write*."[2]

---

[2] "What is implied here [in the old formula, "She who writes well 'writes like a man'"]," Trinh T. Minh-ha posits,

> is her capability to write and think differently from other women who, wallowing in confessions and in personal, narcissistic, or neurotic accounts, are held to be hopelessly inept for either objective, subjective, or universal—that is to say accurate—thinking. Remember, the *minor*-ity's voice is always personal; that of the *major*-ity, always impersonal. Logic dictates. Man *thinks*, woman *feels*. (27-28)

Here is a partial list of the topics and qualities of her award-winning stories, according to Watkins herself: Unflinching. Sex. Old men with hard-ons.

That's what makes great literature?

It's how you break in, anyway, if the name below the title of your work betrays you as a member of the female sex. It's how you build a career.

And the boyfriend, did he not want that for me?

I wish you had a different hobby, he told me once. *I'm* a writer, he said. I'm already thinking about writing. I don't want you talking about writing, reminding me about writing.

So, with him too, I stopped talking.

It was a period of prolonged silence. It was part of my degree in being a woman writer.

The year after my first story was published, Goldwater selected a few other students' stories for his journal, including the infatuated guy's. When his story appeared in print, I congratulated him. He shrugged: "Who cares?" But he'd cared when it was my story, and not his, being published.

"I don't think you have a big head," his childhood friend, who'd met up with a group of us, had told me privately one night in a booth at the bar.

"My head is large?" I asked, bringing my hands to my skull, not at first understanding.[3]

---

[3] Minh-ha:

> To point out that, in general, the situation of women does not favor literary productivity is to imply that it is almost impossible for them (and especially for those bound up with the Third World) to engage in writing as an occupation without their letting themselves be consumed by a deep and pervasive sense of guilt. . . . The circle in which they turn proves to be vicious. . . . Doubts, lack of confidence, frustrations, despair: these are sentiments born with the habits of distraction, distortion, discontinuity, and silence. (7)

And a year later: "Have you considered," Goldwater asked during our thesis meeting, "a PhD in literature?" This was after *I have a crush on you.* After *I didn't think you were very bright.*

"You'd make a fine literary critic," he observed, though he'd never read my critical work.

"Of course," he added, an afterthought, "your writing is also good."

Not much effort put forth to sound convincing.

Then he abruptly ended our meeting, sent me on my way.

Outside his office, heart stretched thin, I leafed through the pages of my thesis, looking for his written comments. I didn't find a single pen mark.

Here she is again: undeserving.

*

Many years later, during my first teaching position in a small town in Colorado, a visiting writer, with whom the faculty in the English department were having dinner, asked me: "How far along are you?" He meant my pregnancy. I was a stick carrying a medicine ball. "That soon?" he said. "I wouldn't have guessed." He meant it as a compliment. "And you?" he asked my husband—also a writer, the chair had said as he introduced us (though, unlike me, he added, Val wasn't a faculty member). "What are you working on?"

My husband, seated across from him, put down his fork. "A memoir." Reluctant. "It was my dissertation. I'm still revising it. But Jen," he brought the conversation back to me, sitting beside the big-shot writer (another septuagenarian, as it happened), "just finished her novel."

"Your dissertation?" the big shot persisted. "What's it about?"

"Oh," Val said, "my uncle." He sighed. "Actually, I haven't looked at it in a while. I've been getting our place ready for the baby." Then he gestured at me again. "But Jen's book—you want to explain it, honey?"

"Um," I started.

"Can't find the time, huh?" The writer shook his head at my husband. "A shame."

I picked up my burger, filled my mouth with meat.

At the other end of the table: another man who didn't think I deserved my job. He took advantage of the lull in the conversation to slide a copy of one of his own novels, published by a friend, to the visiting writer. "A gift!" he said over the restaurant noise.

I wondered how he chose, from his many self-touted books, this one.

If he could, without anyone but the famous writer and me hearing it, my former colleague would have added: "Why don't you give him your book, Jen? Oh, that's right. Never mind." But other faculty members were present. He wasn't a fool.

When it was just the two of us, my colleague liked to tell me about the woman I replaced, who got a better job elsewhere and who, I'm guessing, hated him:

"She didn't even have a fucking book."

As in, What right did she have? to not bite her tongue.

In private, he also liked to say (on seven, eight occasions) about the people on the search committee who selected me: "Can you believe they didn't choose him?" *Him* being a candidate for my job. Sighing and rolling his eyes as he said it, as if naturally I'd agree how stupid it was, passing that man up—a writer, my colleague never failed to add, who was a finalist for a major book prize now. When I didn't even *have* a book. He didn't say this last part; it was understood.

My colleague met the other candidate at a conference soon after I'd started—had bonded with him, he also confided in me, over the idiocy of the hiring. Were now friends.

He told me all manner of things in private.

How, for instance, there were *a lot* of women in our department. (The ratio, I didn't point out, of women to men, wasn't quite half.) How he could get my book published; he had friends. How so-and-so didn't have a book, might not get tenured. How that's probably why the chair had assigned me more service responsibilities—he was worried about *my* tenure prospects.

My colleague also asked me, as I might a student, if I'd ever been to AWP, our nation's largest writers' conference. He flipped through a journal in which a story of mine appeared and said patronizingly, "Isn't it nice, doesn't it feel good, seeing your work in print?"

Soon, I noticed a change in some of my colleagues, his friends. In a meeting, I asked one of them how many incoming students we could expect. "They were all asking to work with you, Jen," he said. "Oh?" I asked, confused, then caught myself. Of course not: his joke. He smirked.

That the person who frequently communicated to me that I didn't deserve my job would say the same to my colleagues wasn't surprising. I did, however, wonder what he told my students. Once or twice, on my way to the bathroom, I'd heard him say my name while he met with a student in his office. By the time I passed his open door, however, he was whispering.

That winter, my passive-aggressive colleague invited the man he claimed should have my job—someone who, he finally admitted once, didn't make it to the first round of interviews—to campus. If I tell you that the unofficial theme of the event was, Can You Believe They Hired Jen Instead of Him? perhaps you can appreciate the dread I felt, panic. Going back on the job market. Instead of reworking again and sending out again the novel my husband had earlier mentioned to the hotshot septuagenarian writer. Who, as we parted ways outside the restaurant, had smiled at my belly: "Good luck with the baby." In the breast pocket of his jacket: my colleague's book.

It's true I still haven't published a book. It's also true I worked for years and years on that novel, reworked it and reworked it and reworked it. Sent it out—hundreds of agents, small presses, contests. Had a few bites, was a finalist for book awards. But here's the problem as I see it: I'm a woman.

"This is certainly publishable," editors from presses wrote while passing on publishing it.

"Brilliant," some said, "but."

"I couldn't connect with the protagonist," agents who'd asked for the full manuscript said after reading it, "emotionally."

Francine Prose asks, "Is the difficulty, fundamentally, that all readers…approach works by men and women with different expectations? It's not at all clear what it means to write 'like a man' or 'like a woman,' but perhaps it's still taken for granted, often unconsciously and thus insidiously, that men write like men and women like women—or at least they should."

Here is what I did wrong.

I wrote a challenging, footnoted, experimental novel. A book no one wants to read—least of all if it's written by a woman. We might occasionally tolerate the cerebral, the experimental, but only if DFW writes it. If Pynchon. Danielewski. Women are meant to move us, emotionally.

And if they don't, they'd better show us some of that good old-man-Watkins-dick.

Prose again:

> Another charge often leveled at women writers is that our work is limited to the rather brief run "between the boudoir and the altar." Men write sweeping, phone-book-size sagas of the big city, social class, of our national destiny, our technological past and future. They produce boldly experimental visionary fiction that periodically revives the moribund novel. Women write diminutive fictions, which take place mostly in interiors, about little families with little problems.

But, as Prose deftly demonstrates through a series of anonymously excerpted novels and stories, such distinctions are themselves a fiction.

Even if that fiction leads to all too real consequences.

My husband suggests I use a nom de plume, like George Eliot, George Sand. Or my initials. Like J. K. Rowling. Not bad advice—but it wouldn't work, not for that novel. Another problem: overtly feminist themes. Dead giveaway.

But perhaps my work is simply crap? I ask myself that all the time, all. The. Time.

If you google Catherine Nichols, you'll find articles about an experiment she conducted. She sent a query with sample pages of her novel to fifty agents. Two requested her full manuscript. Then she sent the identical materials to another fifty agents from a different email address, this time using the pseudonym, "George." Now it was requested *seventeen* times, including by an agent who'd rejected it earlier. "He is eight and a half times better than me at writing the same book," she notes about "George" in her essay for *Jezebel*. "My novel wasn't the problem, it was me—Catherine."

The trouble is you start to believe them: I *am* the loser my colleague advertised to other faculty and probably my students. I *didn't* deserve that job—or especially this second, better one. I still don't have a book. I don't *deserve* a book.

After rewriting again and again, you send what must be a shitty book to shitty presses. The kind that misspells your name in their list of finalists. The kind that would have, if they had published it, inserted their errors all throughout your intricate, painstaking work, years and years and years.

So you stop sending it out. Nowhere, you tell yourself, is better than there.

For the second novel, you go back to your roots: men misbehaving. What Goldwater taught you. Maybe, you tell yourself, they'll like this one. Maybe you can save your career.

But here—another problem: you can't help yourself. Anger seeps into its pages. If there is anything more repellent than an unemotional woman, it's this: a critical one. It won't sell. "Virginia Woolf," Prose points out, "was hardly the first to speculate about why men seem less than thrilled to hear the truth from women." She quotes Woolf:

> And it serves to explain how…impossible it is for her to say to them this book is bad, this picture is feeble… without giving far more pain and rousing far more anger than a man would do who gave the same criticism.

That former colleague of mine? The micro-aggressor. You've never met a person more sensitive or quick to take offense.

When I'd said I didn't submit to my doctoral program's literary journal because I worried it might seem suspect to others if it were published, he assumed I meant *him*. I'd said *I*, but what I really must have meant was the story *he'd* published in *his*. Never mind that I hadn't known about the publication he was now busy defending (or could hardly find fault in it, my first story having been published, after all, by my professor). I didn't scrutinize his CV, as he clearly did mine, citing back to me, at faculty parties, various items from it: "You only have the one critical piece published, though, right?" You've never met a person more obsessed.

Of course he'd assume malice, when everything from him, when no one else was around, was laden with barbed wire or calculated to sabotage. "Do you think you might be presenting at too many conferences, Jen?" "You don't have to participate in the faculty reading series." "Can I be honest? As a friend? You should speak up more in department meetings."

And more fatherly advice: "You should promote yourself more. If not, people might…"

Believe what you tell them?

If one were brave enough to look long enough, if one could have stomached it, one would have seen, in those sunken eyes, a dream: to crush me.

*

Who was I, after all, to have gotten that job—when he, too, something he never said, even in private, had interviewed for it? ("I don't hold any grudges," he did say, once, when I started. "I understand why they picked you—you write nonfiction." I didn't. "You publish a lot of critical work, then." Not that, either.) Who was I, writing "confessional fiction," a term he coined during the Q&A after our faculty reading because—?

He reached for a descriptor and couldn't come up with anything that existed?

Here's one: *autobiographical fiction*. He must have known that one. How many white men, after all, a demographic of writers I knew for sure he taught, have worked in that mode?

Many, many, many.

But if what he hoped to communicate was something about female writers, in particular, he might have selected this more recent term: *autofiction*. Synonym for autobiographical fiction but used more often for work written by women and including a note of derision. Because, as we all know, when a woman uses her life as inspiration, it's because she lacks imagination. When Hemingway, Joyce, Kerouac, Baldwin, Capote, Wolfe, Roth, O'Brien, or Sebald does it, it's genius. Genre bending.

"The novel," David Shields writes in *Reality Hunger: A Manifesto*, "has always been a mixed form; that's why it was called *novel* in the first place." He continues:

> A great deal of realistic documentary, some history . . . barely disguised autobiography have always been part of the novel, from Defoe through Flaubert and Dickens. . . . I see writers like Naipaul and Sebald making a necessary postmodernist return to the roots of the novel as an essentially Creole form, in which "nonfiction" material is ordered, shaped, and imagined as "fiction." (14)

Postmodernist: another term—used here to describe novels (all by men, of course) that sound, I can't help noticing, an awful lot like those written by Sheila Heti, Jenny Offill, Rachel Cusk, Chris Krauss. Writers whose works have been labeled autofiction even as they reject the term.

Auto. Fiction. Like autofellatio, but without the erect penis.

But maybe it didn't satisfy our micro-aggressor, *autofiction*, didn't fully capture it?

Confessional.

Whenever he applied the word to poetry—the well-established style—he scoffed, rolled his eyes. He might as well have said *trauma, sexual abuse.* Such trivial, tawdry things. Privately, he spoke disparagingly of our students who wrote about such matters. From our conversations, I quickly gathered that he didn't think much of memoir, either. But he was hardly the first writer I'd heard dismiss the genre. My students, too, had absorbed these biases, considered using their own lives in their stories to be a form of "cheating," equivalent to lifting the material from their diaries wholesale. But hadn't I also doubted myself, worried my work was solipsistic?[4] Artless, critics say. Why should anyone care about our experiences? Humdrum, sordid. Navel-gazing.

"I'm finished," Febos asserts, "referring in a derogatory way, to stories of body and sex and gender and violence and joy and childhood and family as navel-gazing" (4–5).[5]

Myself, I'm finished tolerating it.

I'm finished biting my tongue, protecting their egos (and myself—from the retaliation I fear).

I'm finished with practiced deafness, dumbness.

Goodbye to all that.

---

[4] "Since when," Melissa Febos asks in *Body Work,* "did telling our own stories and deriving their insights become so reviled?"

> It doesn't matter if the story is your own, I tell [my students] over and over, only that you tell it well. Should we not always tell stories so that their specificity reveals some larger truth? ... Tell me: who is writing in their therapeutic diary and then dashing it off to be published? I don't know who these self-indulgent (and extravagantly well-connected) narcissists are. But I suspect that when people denigrate them in the abstract, they are picturing women. (4)

[5] "This charge," Eula Biss notes in a roundtable discussion with Sarah Manguso and Maggie Nelson, "is sometimes extended to anything written in the first person, a charge of 'navel-gazing.'"

> This also somewhat solidifies an often vaguer association between memoir and the body, and then the frequent efforts to position memoir as low art or "artless." ... [All of which] intersect on occasion with woman-hating, another cultural feature. (Rowbottom)

Goodbye, professor from the theatre department who used the Q&A portion of a faculty reading to ask if the literary journal from which I'd just read my published story was my diary. "You're asking," I tried to clarify in the fog of huh? circling my brain, "if this"—I held the print journal up by its spine, so that he, in the audience, could see its cover—"is my private diary?"

He nodded.

Here I am, David Shields. I confess. *Splintering. Exploding.*
Is this *embarrassing?*
Does it all seem *underprocessed, underproduced?* (27). Raw. Unrefined. Gauche.
Does it? to you.

Hybrid writing. Memoir in fragments. Nonfiction stories. Lyrical essays. Confessionalism. Let's discuss the myriad ways in which these forms have been gendered and, consequently, pilloried.
Let's not.[6]

Instead, consider postcolonial theorist Homi Bhabha's concept of hybridity: "When they make these intercultural, hybrid demands," he writes in *The Location of Culture*, "the natives are both challenging the boundaries of discourse and subtly changing its terms by setting up another specifically colonial space of the negotiations of cultural authority" (169).[7]

---

[6] For an excellent discussion of this, see Rowbottom's "The 'F-Word': Fragmentation and the Futility of Genre Classification: A Roundtable Discussion with Eula Biss, Sarah Manguso, Maggie Nelson, and Allie Rowbottom."

[7] As Bill Ashcroft, et. al., argue in *The Empire Writes Back: Theory and Practice in Post-Colonial Literatures,*

Women in many societies have been relegated to the position of 'Other', marginalized and, in a metaphorical sense, 'colonized',

Hybridity, Bhabha writes, is "at once a mode of appropriation and of resistance" (172).

It is "the name for the strategic reversal of the process of domination through disavowal (that is, the production of discriminatory identities that secure the 'pure' and original identity of authority)" (159). "Then, as discrimination turns into the assertion of the hybrid, the insignia of authority becomes a mask, a mockery" (172).[8] Hybridity is "*less than one and double*" (166).

It is a "space in between the rules of engagement" (277).

Eula Biss: "I've never found the taxonomy of genre particularly accurate and there is something about it that feels … um, like a charmingly pointless pastime? Maybe even a little colonialist and slightly macabre, like the pinning of butterflies. And maybe a tad gendered, too?" (Rowbottom).

Consider, as well, Trinh T. Minh-ha:

> Can any one of us write *like* a man, *like* a woman, *like* a white? Surely, someone would quickly answer, and this leads us straight back to the old master-servant's Guilt. A sentence-thinker, yes, but one who so very often does not know how a sentence will end, I say. And as there is no need to rush, just leave it open, so that it may later

forced to pursue guerrilla warfare against imperial domination from positions deeply imbedded in, yet fundamentally alienated from, that *imperium* (Spivak 1987). They share with colonized races and peoples an intimate experience of the politics of oppression and repression, and like them have been forced to articulate their experiences in the language of their oppressors. (172)

[8] "[L]ike post-colonial criticism, feminist criticism has now turned… towards a questioning of forms and modes, to unmasking the assumptions upon which such canonical constructions are founded, moving first to make their cryptic bases visible and then to destabilize them" (Ashcroft 173).

on find, or not find, its closure. Words, fragments, and lines that I love for no sound reason; blanks, lapses, and silences that settle in like gaps of fresh air as soon as the inked space smells stuffy. (19)

Splintering. Exploding.[9]

A threat to Order. Purity. Authority.

Shields: "'Lyric essay' is a rather ingenious label, since the essayist supposedly starts out with something real, whereas the fiction writer labors under a burden to prove, or create, that reality."
   Supposedly. Whereas.[10]
   "The implied secret," Shields continues, "is that one of the smartest ways to write fiction today is to say that you're not, and then to do whatever you very well please. Fiction writers, take note. Some of the best fiction is now being written as nonfiction" (26).
   Whatever you very well please.

If only this were fiction. If only I'd called it non.

*

---

[9] "In the evaluation of post-colonial literatures it is the centre which imposes its criteria as universal, and dictates an order in terms of which the cultural margins must always see themselves as disorder and chaos" (Ashcroft 186).

[10] "A 'privileging norm' was enthroned at the heart of the formation of English Studies as a template for the denial of the value of the 'peripheral', the 'marginal', the 'uncanonized'. Literature was made as central to the cultural enterprise of Empire as the monarchy was to its political formation. So when elements of the periphery and margin threatened the exclusive claims of the centre they were rapidly incorporated" (Ashcroft 3-4).

In "On Pandering," Watkins cites Rebecca Solnit's famous essay, "Men Explain Things to Me," referencing her by now well-known continuum. It stretches from *too skinny* to *I have a crush on you* to *You don't deserve your job* to *underprocessed* (underestimated), *underproduced* (undervalued) to assault to, yes, murder. And of all kinds. Of confidence, of career, of identity.

My story is my story, but it is also yours. It bends time and snakes between continents and sits at this table and in that office and on a screen. It opens its mouth and tells you—at a bar, perhaps:

"You're not that good-looking."

As this man visiting his friends in South Korea did, while I (twenty-two, a baby) ordered a drink. "I don't get it." He shook his head, appalled. "What are they talking about?"

Who was he? I'd never seen him before.

A responsible citizen—that's who. Letting this big-headed girl know that a) she's ugly, and b) his friends were somehow blind to it. Knocking her back to her rightful place, like she *deserved*. As if she'd had any idea, at all, about his friends until that moment. As if it were her fault, something she'd done, or asked for, instead of something being done to her right now.

A girl who liked to hang out in bars with her friends and talk and laugh and drink and dance. And who ought, apparently, to know better by now—twenty-six, was she then? During her MFA.

"You dance how I imagined," the infatuated guy who was growing more bitter by the day emailed to tell her. "No rhythm." The night before, she'd gone out with some classmates and—recalling a time when she'd felt, dancing with a friend (lost to breast cancer now) in a deserted bar, carefree, joyful—she jumped and twirled. When she looked up, she saw the boy at the edge of the crowd (who had invited him?), his hands deep in his trench-coat pockets, watching her.

"You're a terrible dancer," he made sure to let her know in his email the next morning.

And still, all these years later, this is what she feels: guilty.

(Un)deserving.

Angry.

"Maybe don't come out with us," a mutual friend in our MFA program advised me once. "It just encourages him." What she meant was stay home. Don't have any friends, a life. For two years, his infatuation thrived. I'd told him all along I had a boyfriend. He knew the boyfriend. It didn't matter. What I should have told him was I wouldn't have dated him, even without the boyfriend. At the time, I'd thought saying so gratuitous. I'd thought to spare his ego.

Of that, I am guilty.

He sent an email, finally, blaming me for his going back on anti-depressants.

Then, at long last, he found a girlfriend.

That semester, he submitted for workshop a story featuring a two-page description of a pair of enormous breasts into which the narrator greedily submerges his face again and again.

Revenge always takes the same unoriginal shapes.

"Like *you* don't care," his friend in our MFA program had told me when we were at the bar one night after his story had been panned in workshop, "that you're flat chested." Sucker punch. I'd just joined the booth, heard the end of his conversation, said: "Women don't care about penis size." Momentarily forgetting myself—that I, flat-chested/not a *real* woman should shut the fuck up.

Who was I, after all, to comment? Who was I to have my own work praised, and published, or to be the object of his friend's persistent crush?

"You have no boobs," a fellow ESL teacher in South Korea had told me a couple of years earlier, "like," he added, "at all." This was after he'd called me into his office and stared at his computer screen as he asked why he and I didn't date. Was he joking? I'd wondered. His eyes were still on the spreadsheet. We called him BJ—his initials—because he was constantly talking about sex. "I wouldn't get involved with a coworker," I'd said cautiously. "This town is too small." Trying not to betray my panic, I added, "I wouldn't date anyone who lives here." Earlier that semester, as I'd walked up the campus hill to our building, he'd said, from behind: "You lost your ass." It was right after I'd spent nine weeks traveling in Southeast Asia. "But you have," he argued with the screen now, "you have dated men in town." So I changed tacks: "Why would you want to settle down with me and give up all that Korean pussy?" Mimicking him. He chuckled: "You make a good point."

And, done with me, he kicked me out of his office. Then told me, days later, that I had no boobs.

Who was I, small breasted, not that good looking, or bright, to not fall on my knees, thank them?

Guilt. How many women are made to feel it? Guilt for not returning feelings. Guilt for leading a man on. Guilt for taking his job. Taking his publication. Guilt for wanting a seat at the table. For daring to be ambitious. For her successes. For spending time away from family to achieve them.

On her, we call this look *Selfish. Ugly. Repellent.* On him, *Dashing. Aspirational. Triumphant.*

Accused of *wallowing in confessions*, if a woman also writes autobiography, she is "a monster," her motives for drawing from her life attributed to a crude "desire for revenge" and to "puff an ego already inflated past safety" (Febos 5–6). Thank god, then, for men. Putting her in her place.

Avenging themselves.

It's shameful, she's told—committing to the page what he did, confessed.

And helping to deflate the writer's ego: another woman. *Not plausible. Not a very good story.* Her success undeserved. "By convincing us to police our own and one another's stories," Febos contends, "they have enlisted us in the project of our continued disempowerment" (20-21).

"There's nothing innovative here," the infatuated guy proclaimed after it was my turn to share a writing exercise that we'd been assigned for a course on narrative fiction structures my third semester. He waved the page at me. A woman beside him nodded and declared: "It's pat."

"It's just a dumb exercise," I muttered—though I'd labored over that page. Who'd said it had to be innovative? Was *his* piece innovative? It had a strong voice, we'd said—because of his run-on sentences. The assignment had required us to use the professor's list of words—butterfly, net, I can't remember what else—in a scene. "It's well written," she said kindly now, despite my having criticized her exercise. I felt embarrassed—for betraying her. For betraying my emotions.

Most of my writing drew from my life, but this I'd written from a man's perspective. He was on a plane, he was hitting on a woman, he was calling her a butterfly, he was trapping her in his metaphorical net. It was bad, I think. Pat. My work, as I said, was usually autobiographical.

But it was fiction, I always insisted. (Something to hide behind, perhaps?)

I didn't know about creative nonfiction, and there was no one telling me, as there is now,

> It is not gauche to write about trauma. It is subversive. The stigma of victimhood is a timeworn tool of oppressive powers to gaslight the people they subjugate into believing that by naming their disempowerment they are being dramatic, whining, attention-grabbing, or else beating a dead horse. (Febos 20)

It isn't serious literature, they say. Shopworn. We've seen it before. Why should we care?

As if that were the only reason one reads stories.

For their innovation.

And yet. You've always been a good student, haven't you? Learned their lessons. Applied them.

Hence: that first experimental novel.

Unpublishable.

*

More recently, a student of mine (let's call him A) submitted a paper titled, "White Male: The Last Minority." He was responding to the chapter "Commitment from the Mirror-Writing Box" I'd assigned from Minh-ha's *Woman, Native, Other*, in which she describes the "triple bind" a woman writer of color faces, bound as she is "to go through the ordeal of exposing her work to the abuse of praises and criticisms that either ignore, dispense with, or overemphasize her racial and sexual attributes." Again and again, she is made to choose:

> Writer of color? Woman writer? Or woman of color? Which comes first? Where does she place her loyalties? On the other hand, she often finds herself at odds with language, which partakes in the white-male-is-norm ideology and is used predominantly as a vehicle to circulate established power relations. . . . As focal point of cultural consciousness and social change, writing weaves into language the complex relations of a subject caught between the problems of race and gender and the practice of literature as the very place where social alienation is thwarted differently according to each specific context. (6)

In writing her hybrid, multimedia scholarly book, Minh-ha, as I saw it, was forging new ground, opening a non-binary space in which she herself might exist.

In the chapter I'd assigned, she describes, as well, the rejection that female writers grow accustomed to in a publishing industry that frequently uses the adjective "lady" as shorthand for bad (*lady* writer), a bias, she adds, that's more pronounced for women of color.

But what about *me*? Student A essentially demanded.

He was a doctoral student. It was the last week of a seminar that had on its reading list novels and scholarly essays by predominantly male writers, many of them white. And yet he took issue with having to read one short text that focused exclusively on female writers of color.

Didn't white-male writers also struggle? he persisted. Why doesn't she mention that?

Why, I asked, would she need to? Is there a dearth of work and scholarship by and about them? (And, I might have added, I don't recall your minding, in the other texts we read this semester, the absence of any mention of women of color.) Then I stumbled into a clumsy *Black Lives Matter* analogy: Only certain lives have been devalued to such a degree as to necessitate such a bald reminder. Only certain writers are made to feel they need to ask permission to write.

Gloria Anzaldúa writes, "How dare I even consider becoming a writer?" in "Speaking in Tongues: A Letter to 3rd World Women Writers." She continues: "Does not our class, our culture as well as the white man tell us writing is not for women such as us?" (164).

Lady writer. *Chicana* writer.

Q: What is a white male writer called?

A: Writer.

"The *lesbian* of color," Anzaldúa posits, "is not only invisible, she doesn't even exist. Our speech, too, is inaudible" (163).

And whenever she tries to exist, there's the white man again, demanding she move over and cede her space to him: What about *me*?

For that seminar, I'd paired Minh-ha with Gayl Jones' *Eva's Man.* Student A found the novel—about a Black woman essentially trapped in a room by a dominating man and (via her memories) by a series of abusive men from her childhood to adulthood—*disturbing, difficult.* (I wondered why he hadn't, on the other hand, expressed discomfort earlier that semester when we'd covered Colson Whitehead's *The Underground Railroad* in which slaves are beaten, raped, and murdered.)

Because I'd read my students' responses before class, I came prepared with statistics and Francine Prose's "Scent of a Woman's Ink," from which we read excerpts.

What, Student A interrupted me, is she complaining about? "Look at Toni Morrison," he said—the lone woman of color on the lists I'd passed out of Pulitzer Prize for Fiction and Nobel Prize in Literature winners over the past century. One out of a hundred was apparently plenty.

"And what about J. K. Rowling?" he added. "Best-selling author of all time." Then he folded his arms. Mic drop.

"Commercial," I said—though I might have asked instead why he thought she'd been told to use J. K. rather than Joanne. "Young adult. Prose, remember, is identifying trends in *literary* fiction."

Then came the onslaught of student objections: *Harry Potter* isn't literature?

We were getting off track.

"Did that determine," Student A's buddy jumped into the fray, "what books you selected for our course—the *gender* of the writers?"

"Unfortunately, no," I said—which seemed to take the wind from his sails. Apparently, A's buddy had not only failed to notice how poor a job I'd done of equally representing women in my own seminar, he'd felt it (a 10:4 ratio, male to female) to be over-representative of female writers. "I'll be more mindful next time," I added, pretending to misinterpret the intention of his question. Then I read aloud, anonymously, as I'd done all semester, "White Male: The Last Minority."

Hearing the title, one of the women chuckled. ("I thought, at first," she later explained, "it was a parody.") When I finished reading, I looked at the students at the seminar table.

The room pulsed its displeasure.

"All I have to say," a woman, usually reticent, spoke up, "is that whoever wrote that…" She shook her head and grumbled something unintelligible.

"It wasn't *my* response paper," Student A's buddy said, unable to help himself.

"I have data," the woman who'd laughed said. "The VIDA Count. I'll send it around."

The next morning, Student A emailed: he wanted to meet to clear the air. He was upset.

On the surface, all that had happened was I'd provided context for Minh-ha's essay and read aloud his response, as I always did. He'd gotten what he wanted, then, hadn't he? Or was I supposed to read it aloud without comment? Each time he'd interrupted me, was I not supposed to comment then either? Was it not a dialogue? Were the other students merely his audience members? Had he imagined his argument so convincing when he wrote his response that uttering his words would silence us all? Whatever the trouble was, he wanted to meet. To clear the air.

It was my responsibility, I saw, to reassure and coddle him. A man in his late thirties.

As a new, untenured faculty member myself, at a university that would appraise my teaching (read: my student course evaluations) as critically as my research, I obliged him.

Bit my tongue.

You have it hard, yes. Your feelings are valid.

As opposed to mine. As opposed to your classmates'. As opposed to Minh-ha's.

In his evaluation of my teaching, Student A wrote at notable length about what he took to be the shortcomings of the course, citing *Eva's Man* as an example—not that he disdained women writers of color or reading about their unsavory experiences, but that it wasn't as "experimental" as the professor thought, not as experimental as, for instance (schooling his teacher), *The House of Leaves*. Betraying once more, in this way, the depth and persistence of his misunderstandings.

Encountering that semester such works as Vladimir Nabokov's *Pale Fire* (which A treated unmaliciously as toilet reading, flipping through and skimming its pages at random, as if the writer hadn't put much thought into its order) and Manuel Puig's *Kiss of the Spider Woman* (which A, an unpublished writer himself, attempted to workshop in our narrative theory course, making suggestions for how this writer he'd never heard of, Puig whoever, could improve his little novel)—A had concluded, reading such texts, that the primary purpose of our seminar was to study experimentation. That isn't, I'd told him, point blank, multiple times, our objective. I'd said (citing David Foster Wallace, who'd in fact referenced *Kiss of the Spider Woman* as a prime example) that the shape of a novel—its narrative methods and form—should be determined by its content. One ought to feel, as one reads it, a sense that it couldn't have been written any other way. Experimentation was beside the point, I stressed again, and would lead to a dead end in our discussions. Narrative, I said: Keep your focus there. How does *that* dictate form?

"I've seen footnotes in novels before," he declared about *Kiss of the Spider Woman*, minutes after I'd delivered a version of the above speech, again. "This isn't new."

Who said it was supposed to be? (Puig's novel, by the way? was written in 1976.)

I referenced Shields—what he says about the origins of the novel. Mentioned *Tristram Shandy* (1759). Though some of the novels we were reading that semester, I pointed out, might be labeled unconventional within the current trends, they were not, in fact, doing anything new.

"Nicholson Baker," Student A said as if I hadn't spoken, "uses footnotes. For instance."

"*The Mezzanine*," I said. "Yep."

"*Oscar Wao*," Student A's buddy added, "has footnotes." Then asked if I'd heard of it. A novel he'd read for the first time the previous semester. A novel that featured largely in a critical piece I'd published five years earlier.

"You do realize, of course," I said, "that those novels were likely influenced by Puig's?"

"Doesn't *Infinite Jest*," Student A blithely asked his buddy, "also have footnotes?"

"*Gravity's Rainbow*—" his friend changed the subject, "*that's* a good novel. Pynchon."

"Endnotes," I said in case anyone was listening. "Can we get back to *Spider Woman*?"

A typical exchange that semester.

The week before his dissertation defense, Student A emailed me instructions for how to run it, a bullet-point list of the order in which to proceed. When I replied matter-of-factly with the correct procedures to which I'd be adhering, he replied: Sorry if I offended you.

As in: I didn't mean to get you all worked up.
Easy, honey. Whoa, whoa.
I was just telling you how to do your job.

*

"A canon," Bill Ashcroft, et. al., instruct us in *The Empire Writes Back*,

> is not a body of texts *per se*, but rather a set of reading practices (the enactment of innumerable individual and community assumptions, for example about genre, about literature, and even about writing).... [T]he subversion of a canon involves the bringing-to-consciousness and articulation of these practices. (186)

What about other canons? Ones outside the strictly textual?

Do my male colleagues, I sometimes wonder, for instance, get unsolicited advice from students? Do their students expect to be shown leniency and given special dispensations? *Raise my grade. My absences shouldn't count. I need an extension.* Do my colleagues receive emails without a salutation (or addressed to Mr. instead of Professor or Dr.), in which inappropriate demands on their time and emotional reserves are made? *Here. Proofread this* [fill in the blank]. And if they are indeed treated like this and consequently refer students to the university's services devoted to such activities, Academic & Career Planning, or the Writing Center, are they met with hostility? *I guess you don't care.* Do they spend hours responding to a student's emails half a dozen times, encouraging him (forever threatening revolt or breakdown), only to receive another email with no salutation: "Mechanical errors? What do you mean? Do you think I didn't spend time on my story? I did! Don't you like it? You can't make a statement like that, mechanical errors, and then leave me hanging!" And, if these and other demands aren't met to his satisfaction (*My mistake. You're a genius. Forget grammar*), must they read subsequent rage-filled stories involving the narrator shooting in the forehead an adversary or being forced to submit to the "Irascible Queen" and her arbitrary rules? Does the student slump at his desk, arms folded for the rest of the term? Do my colleagues fear walking on campus after that night class? Do their course evaluations feature comments like *For someone as young as him, I thought he'd be more understanding?*

Probably they do, right?

Probably it isn't any different. Probably I'm just paranoid. Probably.

Other probabilities—we've all heard them: 1 in 5. 1 in 4. 81%.

This was originally twice as long. A wise editor read it. "Cut," she advised me. "Keep it to a few illustrative examples. It rings true," she noted, "but all the tales of misogyny, harassment, assault begin to overwhelm, become repulsive."

Solnit's continuum repulsive.

The woman herself: repulsive.

Have I trimmed enough?

Karr, quoting Jerry Stahl, in *The Art of Memoir*: "If you had to live it, you get to write it" (111).

But then again, it is a man saying this.

Surely, *he* wasn't disgusting.

"We victimize the victim," that editor also wrote. "It's unfortunate, but true. Because: people."

She must have asked for it.
Deserved it.

Here is my challenge to you, reader. Make space for alternative possibilities. Disrupt the canon.

Works Cited

Anzaldúa, Gloria. "Speaking in Tongues: A Letter to Third World Women Writers." *This Bridge Called My Back: Writings by Radical Women of Color*, Eds. Gloria Anzaldúa and Cherríe Moraga, SUNY Press, 2015, pp. 163-72.

Ashcroft, Bill, et al. *The Empire Writes Back: Theory and Practice in Post-Colonial Literatures*. 2nd ed., Routledge, 1989.

Bhabha, Homi K. *The Location of Culture*. Routledge, 1994.

Febos, Melissa. *Body Work: The Radical Power of Personal Narrative*. Catapult, 2022.

Karr, Mary. *The Art of Memoir*. Harper Perennial, 2016.

Minh-ha, Trinh T. "Commitment from the Mirror-Writing Box." *Woman, Native, Other: Writing Postcoloniality and Feminism*, Indiana UP, 2009, pp. 5-44.

Nichols, Catherine. "Homme de Plume: What I Learned Sending My Novel Out Under a Male Name." *Jezebel*, 4 Aug. 2015, https://jezebel.com/homme-de-plume-what-i-learned-sending-my-novel-out-und-1720637627.

Prose, Francine. "Scent of a Woman's Ink: Are Women Writers Really Inferior?" *Harper's Magazine*, 1998, https://harpers.org/archive/1998/06/scent-of-a-womans-ink/.

Rowbottom, Allie. "The 'F-Word': Fragmentation and the Futility of Genre Classification: A Roundtable Discussion with Eula Biss, Sarah Manguso, Maggie Nelson, and Allie Rowbottom." *Gulf Coast*, Fall 2011, https://gulfcoastmag.org/journal/25.1/the-f-word/.

Shields, David. *Reality Hunger: A Manifesto*. Vintage, 2010.

Solnit, Rebecca. "Men Explain Things to Me." *Men Explain Things to Me*, Haymarket Books, 2015, pp. 1-15.

Watkins, Claire Vaye. "On Pandering." *Tin House*, 23, Nov. 2015, https://tinhouse.com/on-pandering/.

Acknowledgments

Many of these stories were written during my MFA and PhD. I am grateful to my professors and classmates during those pivotal years. Through their guidance, insights, friendship, and our lively discussions about literature and craft, they helped shape me as a writer, reader, and teacher. I especially wish to thank Brian Trapp, Marjorie Celona, Matt McBride, Linwood Rumney, Tessa Mellas, Brian Brodeur, James Pihakis, Becky Adnot-Haynes, Jason Nemec, Liv Stratman, Mical Darley-Emerson, Ellen Elder, Brenda Peynado, and Ruth Williams. I am particularly indebted to Michael Griffith for his ceaseless generosity as adviser, role model, and ally, as well as to Brock Clarke, Leah Stewart, Jennifer Glaser, Chris Bachelder, Patrick O'Keeffe, and Salar Abdoh for their continued support. I am grateful as well to Myriam J.A. Chancy. Her invaluable lessons, benevolence, and staunch belief in me sustained me then and sustain me now.

I would be remiss if I didn't thank the faculty in the English Department at the University of South Dakota, who have helped me navigate academia, or my graduate students, who inspire and nourish me intellectually and creatively. It's a privilege to work with such talented people.

Many thanks, as well, to the superb editorial and production teams at Cornerstone Press, in particular director & publisher Dr. Ross Tangedal, editors Brett Hill and Grace Dahl, production director Carolyn Czerwinski, and media director Zoie Dinehart.

This book would not exist without the unflagging encouragement and love of my parents, Dan and Wendy McCormack, who instilled in me a reverence for and joy in the arts, nor without my siblings, Maya, Orrin, and Sean, my best friends and veritable safety net, who have selflessly and endlessly given me the confidence and security that has allowed me to take risks in my life. For their partners, who somehow put up with all of us, I am also grateful. I owe special thanks as well to Margo and Rein Vanderhill, who have shown me nothing but love and kindness, and continue to be generous with their hearts as devoted and adoring grandparents.

I will never find enough words to adequately express my gratitude for Dietrik Vanderhill, my love, my life, my partner in everything, constant collaborator and daily source of inspiration, tenderness, rejuvenation, surprise. He performs miracles, continually challenging and motivating this pain in the ass, stubborn, consummate complainer to do and be better. For you and our daughter, Djuna, who has taken up residence in every chamber and lobe of my heart and brain, I will. Thank you.

––––––––––

The following stories first appeared in literary journals:

"Welcome, Welcome, Welcome. Come in. Come in. Come in." (*Redivider*)
"There Are Worse Things" (*South Dakota Review*)
"Conjoined Twins Separated" (*North Dakota Quarterly*)
"Oh, Work!" (*REAL: Regarding Arts & Letters*)
"The Lonely Planet" (*Prairie Fire*)
"Pucka! Pucka! Pucka!" (*The Portland Review*)
"Blameless" (*New England Review*)
"However Broken" (*Hotel Amerika*)
"Fugitive Daydreams" (*Big Muddy*)

Leah McCormack's work has appeared in *New England Review*, *North Dakota Quarterly*, *Redivider*, *Fiction*, *Prairie Fire*, *The Portland Review*, *Hotel Amerika*, *Big Muddy*, and *REAL: Regarding Arts & Letters*. Her unpublished novel, *Contingent Contingencies*, was a finalist for the 2019 AWP Prize for the Novel, the 2018 Nilsen Literary Prize for the Novel, and an honoree for the 2019 Dzanc Books Fiction contest. She teaches creative writing at the University of South Dakota.

www.ingramcontent.com/pod-product-compliance
Lightning Source LLC
Chambersburg PA
CBHW021148190726
48288CB00008B/2874